'You are a visi

Alexa gave him a q

'Is that what you really think?'

The smile had gone and now the look on his face was almost as if he were in pain.

'Yes. You are the most attractive woman in the room, Alexa, and not just because of what you are wearing.'

She smiled up at him. However much it was costing him, and from his expression it was quite a bit, Reece was telling her that she was beautiful.

'So you're seeing me in a different light,' she teased.

'Not necessarily.'

'I'm still seen as the vestal virgin who has to be protected from life's quagmires, am I?'

'Yes, if that's what you are, and if you don't stop teasing I might be tempted to do something to rectify that state of affairs.'

He watched her colour rise in a hot tide and knew that he was throwing caution to the winds after all his vows to do the opposite. She had that effect on him.

Abigail Gordon loves to write about the fascinating combination of medicine and romance from her home in a Cheshire village. She is active in local affairs and is even called upon to write the script for the annual village pantomime!

Her eldest son is a hospital manager and helps with all her medical research. As part of a close-knit family, she treasures having two of her sons living close by and the third one not too far away. This also gives her the added pleasure of being able to watch her delightful grandchildren growing up.

Recent titles by the same author:

EMERGENCY REUNION
SAVING SUZANNAH
THE ELUSIVE DOCTOR

THE NURSE'S CHALLENGE

BY
ABIGAIL GORDON

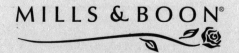

MILLS & BOON and MILLS & BOON with the Rose Device are registered trademarks of the publisher.

First published in Great Britain 2001
Harlequin Mills & Boon Limited,
Eton House, 18-24 Paradise Road, Richmond, Surrey TW9 1SR

© Abigail Gordon 2001

ISBN 0 263 82710 0

Set in Times Roman 10½ on 11½ pt.
03-0102-51681

Printed and bound in Spain
by Litografía Rosés, S.A., Barcelona

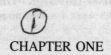

CHAPTER ONE

THERE was a bright summer sun high in the sky and a fresh breeze was ruffling the reeds at the water's edge as Alexa lowered herself onto a nearby rock.

The village of Portinscale had been blessed by the generosity of nature. Lake Derwentwater, big and beautiful, nudged up to it in many places and this was the one she loved the most.

Across the water the bustling Cumbrian town of Keswick would be going about its business on a warm Saturday afternoon, but here all was still.

The white sails of yachts stood out starkly against the distant wooded skyline and nearby, ducks swam past in damp-feathered formation.

Her grandfather, when he'd been alive, had loved this small inlet on the lake shore, and only feet away was the guest house that her sister and brother-in-law owned.

A lively and outgoing twenty-five-year-old, Alexa rarely had a moment to spare, but when she had, it was here that she came.

Lifting her face to the sun's warmth, she closed her eyes, revelling in the silence, and would have extended the pleasurable moment if she hadn't heard the slap of oars against the water and the high tones of young voices.

As she began to focus on the sight in front of her she sighed for the precious peace that was gone.

A rowing boat was being propelled haphazardly towards the centre of the lake by two boys, and seated beside them were two girls of a similar age, urging them on.

There wasn't anything to be alarmed at on the face of it

but as Alexa watched she saw that the boys hadn't mastered the oars and the girls were fooling about.

When one of them stood up the boat wobbled precariously and Alexa bit into her lip. The behaviour of these youngsters was an accident waiting to happen, she thought worriedly.

At that moment, as if to prove her right, one of the youths left the oars and joined his girlfriend in the middle of the boat and over it went, to the accompaniment of alarmed cries.

They were well out into the lake by then and as Alexa watched in horrified dismay the empty boat righted itself, with the heads of its occupants bobbing around in the water beside it.

Relief swept over her as the two girls struck out for the bank, but the boys weren't making such definite movements. One of them was clinging onto the boat and supporting his friend with his other arm.

'Help!' he cried. 'Timmy can't swim!' With the fear in his voice increasing, he added 'And there's something wrapping around my legs. I'm stuck!'

Thankful that she was only wearing a sleeveless top and flimsy cotton skirt, Alexa had flung off the lightweight mules she was wearing and was already wading through the shallows towards them.

'Hold on! I'm coming!' she cried.

After the first ten yards she was swimming with strong, even strokes and as two white faces came up beside her, going in the opposite direction, she cried to the two girls, 'Get help as fast as you can!'

When she reached the boat the lad was trying to push his friend back into it with one arm, but from the looks of the non-swimmer he was unconscious and the deadweight of him was too much for the lad to lift.

He was weeping with fear and as she swam up beside him he cried, 'I'm trapped. Something's got me!'

'You've become entangled in the weeds beneath the water,' she gasped. 'Don't panic. Once we've got your friend back into the boat I'll dive down to see what's holding you. In the meantime, hang on.'

It sounded simple, put like that, but Alexa knew they were in a mess. If the lad lost his grip on the boat he could be dragged under by the weeds, and there was his unconscious friend who'd either hit his head on the side of the boat as it had gone over, or had swallowed a large amount of water.

Would it be wiser to swim back to shore with the lad while the other one clung on, or try to get him into the comparative safety of the boat? she thought desperately. But supposing it overturned again while they were struggling to get him back on board?

'Hold on there!' a voice cried suddenly from not too far away, and Alexa had never heard a more welcome sound.

Another rower was pulling alongside, this time a competent-looking adult male.

He nodded towards the unconscious lad. 'I'll take him on board,' he said briskly. As he manoeuvred his craft into position, he asked, 'What's with the other lad?'

'Tangled in weeds or something similar,' she cried, 'but he's all right for the moment. It's this one that needs help.'

There was cool purpose in the dark eyes above her. 'I'll take him under the armpits and drag him on board while you both keep the boat steady. Right?'

They were more than ready, and as the stranger eased his limp passenger into the bottom of the boat they held on grimly until the craft steadied itself.

As soon as that had been accomplished the man flung off his shirt, ready to dive in, but Alexa was quicker. She was already plunging down beneath the surface of the lake, pushing away the trailing weeds that seemed to be every-where. She'd grabbed a floating oar as she went down and now she was using it to keep them away from herself.

The underwater vegetation was strong and slimy and it took all her strength to free the boy's legs, but in the end she managed it and as he kicked free she surfaced, covered in a mixture of algae and broken grasses.

The man who'd come to the rescue was giving the non-swimmer artificial respiration when she reappeared and he stopped briefly, offering a strong brown arm to lift them on board.

The other lad climbed carefully onto the boat, followed by Alexa.

'I'll take over,' she said quickly. 'You'll be able to row us back to shore more quickly than I can.'

Dark eyes in a tanned face looked up briefly.

'You've had experience in artificial respiration?'

'Yes!' she cried. 'Take the oars!'

After what seemed like a lifetime, although it was prob-ably only seconds, water spurted from the lad's mouth and Alexa and the stranger exchanged relieved glances.

As the youth lay limply coughing and retching Alexa cast a quick glance at the man at the oars. He'd appeared out of the blue just when he'd been needed, and the angel Gabriel himself couldn't have been more welcome.

Who was he? she wondered. His hair was a dark thatch, cut stylishly around a face that she knew she wasn't going to forget in a hurry. Broad shoulders were flexing in and out as he plied the oars while, with trim hips and long legs hunched against the narrow wooden seat, he braced himself against the movement of the boat.

As she turned back to the shivering boys, Alexa was wishing that they had blankets or something similar to put over them, but there was nothing, apart from the stranger's already damp shirt.

'We need an ambulance fast,' he said crisply as they scraped ashore seconds later in the same spot where not so long ago Alexa had been enjoying the peace of a summer afternoon. 'This young fellow needs to go straight to the hospital and the others ought to be checked over. Where's the nearest phone?'

She was about to tell him when one of the girls, who were shivering nearby, quavered, 'A man walking his dog saw us and he's gone to his house to phone for the ambulance.'

'Good,' he said. 'Let's hope it won't be long.' He turned to Alexa. 'You'd better come along with us. You might need a quick check, too.'

'You're going with them?'

He nodded grimly.

'Yes. As they don't appear to be capable of looking after themselves.'

He certainly had a point there.

She shook her head. 'I'm all right. I'd rather go home to change. It's not far away…and as long as you're going to look after them.'

'You can rely on that,' he told her firmly as the noise of a siren broke into the afternoon.

That same dark gaze was on her again and for a ridiculous moment she wished she weren't wet through and covered in algae.

'If you don't want to come with us, make sure you get into a hot bath the moment you've stripped off,' he ordered. 'And if you do start experiencing any after-effects, either follow us or go to your local surgery.'

'Yes,' she said meekly as Timmy began to vomit again.

'So what have we here?' the first paramedic to alight from the ambulance asked, and as the three walking wounded clambered into the vehicle and the one who'd

almost drowned was stretchered in beside them, Alexa
squelched back to where she'd come from.

'There'll be just six in for dinner,' Carol had said as she'd
hovered on the step. 'Do you think you'll be all right?'

Alexa had smiled and given her sister a gentle push in
the direction of the gate.

'Yes. I will be all right,' she'd told her. 'Especially as
you've done everything except actually put the food in the
oven. For goodness' sake, Carol, enjoy your day. It's time
you had a break.' She saw her brother-in-law beckoning
through the open car window. 'Off you go. Tom's getting
impatient.'

Carol had given her a quick hug.

'You're a love, Alexa.' She'd looked up at where white
window frames stood out starkly against grey Cumberland
slate. 'I love this place, but we've been so busy since we
bought it—'

'Carol! Are you coming?' her husband had bellowed, and
with a swish of skirt and the click of high heels on cob-
blestones, she'd gone.

As she went back inside Alexa was smiling. Because
Carol was the eldest and could cook like a dream, she was
always worried when she left her younger sister in charge.

She and Tom had bought the guest house a couple of
years ago, and today Alexa was holding the fort while they
went to a family wedding.

There'd been an invitation for her, too, but she'd made
an excuse not to go. She'd fancied the bridegroom at one
time and didn't think she wanted to watch Tom's brother,
Christopher Barnett, plight his troth to the giggly holiday
rep who'd caught him in her net.

Also there was Carol. If Alexa had accepted the invitation, her sister would have had no one to leave in charge
for the day.

When she'd appeared, wearing a black armband, Carol had eyed her anxiously, but Tom had hooted with laughter.

'That surely isn't for that brother of mine!' he'd said. 'You could have your pick, Alexa. I've not met a guy yet who isn't bowled over the moment he meets you.'

'Excluding yourself, I hope,' his wife had teased.

He'd replied, 'Of course, darling.' And she'd ended up laughing with him.

'It's all right, you guys laughing.' Alexa had said, keeping up the pretence of mourning, 'but you're not the ones on the shelf.'

'Shelf!' they'd howled in united mirth, and she'd had to join in.

Once they'd gone Alexa looked around her. The breakfasts had been cleared away. The chambermaid had made the beds and tidied the rooms. The lad who kept the gardens tidy had been and gone, and the guests had left to pursue their various interests, leaving silence to reign over Craith House.

It would be hours before she was needed in any management capacity, she'd decided. According to Carol, every guest who stayed with them couldn't wait to explore the Cumbrian lakes and mountains.

Derwentwater itself was only a hundred yards away, so on a bright summer morning such as this visitors couldn't get out into the open quickly enough.

The guest house provided bed, breakfast and evening meal, plus any other snacks that might be required. But at that precise moment no one was demanding anything and she went out through the back door to spend a few minutes by the water's edge—never dreaming that her time out there would be prolonged and that she would eventually go back inside soaking wet.

*   *   *

As she did as she was told and soaked in a hot bath, Alexa thought guiltily that Craith House had been getting scant attention for the last couple of hours. It was fortunate that everyone was out, or Carol's and Tom's reputation for service would be going by the board.

She didn't hear a taxi pull up some time later and quick footsteps on the stairs, and when she went down to Reception, scrubbed and clean in a blue linen shift dress, all was quiet.

It was as she was about to ring the hospital regarding the youngsters that a voice at her elbow said, 'I'd like coffee and a slice of Carol's ginger cake, if you don't mind.'

Alexa turned in slow surprise. She'd heard that voice before and it had the same note of brisk authority in it. But if *she* was taken aback, *he* was dumbstruck.

'I don't believe it!' he exclaimed. 'The lady of the lake! What a transformation! Where have you come from? I haven't seen you before at Craith House. Are you new here or something?'

He was firing questions at her like bullets and she brought herself up to her full height, which didn't quite reach his shoulder. If ever there'd been a moment when she'd wanted to impress, this was it.

'I'm in charge for the day. Carol is my sister and she and Tom have gone to a wedding.'

Her eyes were bright. She was being asked to explain her presence, but what about him? Where had *he* materialised from? Was he a guest? She only helped out at weekends so she wasn't always aware of who was staying in the guest house.

'And where have *you* come from?' she questioned.

Dark brows were rising.

'I'm a guest here, of course. Why else would I be requesting food?'

Alexa could feel her colour rising. It took a lot to intimidate her, but this man could do it.

'I see,' she said coolly. 'And you are…?'

'Rowlinson. Reece Rowlinson, and I'm in room number five if you want to check the register.'

'That won't be necessary,' she murmured. 'And if you'd like to go into the lounge I'll bring the coffee and cake to you, but first tell me about those kids. Are they all right? I feel that I should have gone with you.'

'Why, for goodness' sake? You were in no fit state,' he said dismissively. 'Yes, they're all right. The lad who couldn't swim isn't feeling too well and they're going to keep him in for a couple of days to make sure there are no after-effects, but the other featherbrains have all been discharged, conveniently ignoring the fact that some of them could have been drowned if you hadn't been there.'

'And you,' she said generously. 'I was beginning to wonder where it would all end when you appeared.'

He shrugged, as if rescues on the lake were just part of a day's work, and Alexa thought that this man was obviously a cool customer.

When she took what he had asked for into the lounge he was leafing through a magazine, but he put it to one side when she appeared.

As Alexa placed the tray on a table overlooking the lake she was proud of her efforts. A single rose stood in a small cut-glass vase. The coffee was piping hot, with cream and sugar to go with it alongside. But it was the cake that was the masterpiece. A huge slice of the delicious ginger cake so famed in the Lake District reposed on an elegant china plate.

Stepping back, she gave him the smile that was guaranteed to reassure a fretful child or a nervous adult in the surgery and said, 'There will be no charge for this, Mr Rowlinson. It's on the house. If it hadn't been for you the day might have had a less happy ending for some of us.'

He gave a dismissive wave of the hand. 'Not at all.

Please, put it on my account.' Seating himself behind the table, he began to pour.

As she went back to her perch behind the reception desk, Alexa observed him curiously. He was rugged and very handsome in a clean-cut sort of way, she decided. The typical fell walker, yet he wasn't dressed in hiking clothes. His shirt looked expensive, his trousers not off the peg.

Reece Rowlinson must have been aware of her scrutiny as he called across, 'Are you in the hospitality trade, then…the same as your sister?'

Alexa shook her head and the long chestnut swathe of her hair swung gently to and fro. 'No. Not really. I'm in health care.'

Eyes as brown as lakeland cattle were observing her coolly.

'I might have known. You were calm and very efficient out there at the lake. What do you do?'

Pleasure was washing over her. It was nice to be complimented by this very impressive man. He was having a strange effect on her. She felt giddy and reckless.

'I'm a nurse.'

'So you're just filling in here?'

'Yes.'

'Where are you based? Hospital?'

'No. I work at a lakeside practice in Keswick.'

He was pouring a second cup of coffee and for some reason he almost dropped the pot, but his next comment was so bland that she felt his clumsiness couldn't have had anything to do with what she'd just said.

'Really. How nice.'

Alexa wrinkled a pert nose. 'Most of the time it is, but not always. My favourite doctor is retiring and I'm really going to miss him.'

Her voice had trailed off as she wondered why on earth she was telling this stranger about John Hendrix's departure. Maybe it was because she was feeling unsettled about the changes that were coming at the practice.

Next week Bryan Lomas would be the new senior partner. He was an efficient enough doctor, but with absolutely no personality, and next in line to the throne was Rebecca Soames, an icy cool blonde who never flapped no matter what.

Neither of them were her type. But, then, they didn't have to be. Just because she was happy and bouncy, it didn't mean that the people she worked with had to be the same.

At least she had the measure of those two. It was the new locum who was to be with them for a period of six months who would be the unknown quantity. But having seen a few locums come and go, she would take him in her stride.

The fellow who was coming wasn't a trainee, though. He was some high-flying medic who usually worked abroad and was coming back to England for a fallow period before going off on his travels again.

Apparently he'd once lived in the Lake District and knew John Hendrix from way back. The elderly GP had suggested to his partners that they offer him the temporary post and, surprisingly for a man of his experience, he'd accepted.

He was smiling, but for some reason it wasn't reaching his eyes. 'I'll know where to come if I'm taken ill, then.'

'We do see a lot of visitors,' she told him. 'The Lakes are so busy at this time of year and it's amazing how much more prone to accident or illness people are when out of their own environment.'

'Hmm. I can imagine.'

'Are you staying at Craith House long?' she asked, with the politeness of one stranger to another.

'I'm not sure. I'm here for at least a couple of weeks.

That was the arrangement I made with your sister, but it could be for longer if she isn't booked up.'

'If she is, there are plenty of places who take in visitors here in Portinscale,' Alexa told him, ridiculously pleased to hear that he might be around for some time.

The phone rang at that moment—someone wanting to make a booking—and when the deed was done she looked up to find that the man called Reece Rowlinson had gone.

She didn't see him again until the evening meal was about to be served. He passed the kitchen window as they were getting ready to dish up, and when he nodded briefly in her direction Alexa's spirits lifted.

Megan Davies, who came in each evening to help with the meal, was in charge in the kitchen today and it was left to Alexa and a young girl from the village to wait on table.

As they bustled about the dining room she was aware that he was watching her and would have dearly liked to know what was going through his mind.

'Where do you suggest I walk this evening?' he asked of her as she cleared the tables at the end of the meal. 'After this afternoon's episode I think I'll give watersports a miss.'

She shuddered. 'I can understand that.' In answer to his question she went on, 'How about through the fields to Keswick and along to Friar's Crag?'

'Hmm. Maybe. There's a new theatre near the Crag, I'm told. I might have a look what's on. If you hadn't been on duty here maybe you'd have been willing to show me round.'

'Yes, I would,' she told him with her own particular brand of uncomplicated candour. 'But, as we both know, I'm in charge here until Carol and Tom get back and I have a feeling that it could be very late.'

An elderly couple were hovering behind him, obviously with some comment or request to make, and when he turned and saw them he stepped to one side.

By the time she'd sorted out the packed lunch they required for the following day, he was striding off briskly towards the town, with the evening sun glinting on the dark pelt of his hair.

She didn't see him again. Carol and Tom came home full of their day's events and Alexa in turn regaled them with the story of the lake rescue that had involved one of their guests.

When she asked them what they knew of Reece Rowlinson it was very little. As far as they were concerned, he was holidaying alone in the Lake District and that was it.

As she went down the garden to her own small establishment, an outhouse that Tom had renovated and built an extra storey on to accommodate his young sister-in-law, Alexa's thoughts were still centred on the stranger.

What would he be doing at this moment in room number five? she wondered. Sleeping? Reading? Watching TV? *Was* he on holiday...or what?

Did it matter? Those who came to Craith House were just passing through. She was crazy to be getting all steamed up about someone that she'd only met for a matter of minutes, but in what circumstances! She wouldn't forget today in a hurry.

What were his thoughts about it? she wondered. He was obviously a man who took everything in his stride. She found herself smiling. He had asked her to show him round, so he must be aware of her. What a pity she hadn't been able to oblige.

As Alexa surmised about him Reece Rowlinson wasn't even on the premises. He'd paused on his walk back from Keswick and was standing at the lake edge a mile or so away, looking out over the wide expanse of Derwentwater, glistening beneath a yellow moon.

The night was warm and still. So was the water. He could almost hear his heartbeat. This was the peace he'd yearned for amongst the noise and pandemonium of the refugee camps.

So why had he agreed to spend the next six months working when he could have been sailing, walking and lazing around one of the most beautiful parts of England?

The answers were there almost before he'd asked himself the question. One of them was that he would have had too much time to think. To remember the horrors of war and other blights that fell upon mankind.

Then there was the type of man he was. He couldn't put his skills on hold for so long. That was why he'd agreed to help out a friend, deciding that a commitment in the slower, less demanding way of life of the English Lakes would seem like a rest.

The girl at the guest house had been a strange one, he thought as his mind wandered. She'd had beautiful hair in masses of chestnut tendrils, and the clear, bright gaze of those as yet unscathed by life. Yet she was a nurse, for heaven's sake, and anyone in the medical profession had to have seen the worst side of it.

His mouth curved into a smile as he recalled the way she'd behaved in the water and out of it, and had then gone calmly back to her duties at the guest house. If she hadn't been around, those kids could have come well and truly unstuck.

He wondered where she lived. Had she got a place of her own? Or was she resident at Craith House?

As he turned away from the spell of the lake's dark waters Reece had a feeling that he was soon going to find out.

Alexa awoke on Sunday morning with a strange feeling of anticipation, and as she drowsily sought for a reason the memory of what had happened the day before came back to mind.

Normally she saw little of the visitors who stayed at the guest house. She worked at the practice five weekdays and some Saturday mornings, so what went on at Craith House didn't usually overlap into her life, except for occasional waitressing in the dining room at weekends. But yesterday had been different. Carol and Tom had left her in charge and she'd met one of their guests under rather damp conditions.

Would he be around today? she wondered as she showered and dressed. Or had he made plans? No one in their right mind would stay indoors with lakes, mountains and a summer sun high in the sky to tempt them.

'So,' a voice said from behind as she watered the plants around her small abode, 'you're off the hook today, I take it.'

Alexa swung round, her face lighting up at the sound of his voice. If he *was* going out, it was clear that Reece Rowlinson hadn't yet departed, and she wondered if he would repeat his invitation of the night before.

It was a vain hope.

'Today it's my turn to be on the hook,' he said. 'I'm committed to visiting a friend when I could be sailing the lake or exploring the fells.'

'Really? So you know someone in the area, do you?' she questioned politely as the vision faded of herself and this captivating stranger taking a boat out and maybe dining at the isolated hotel at Ladore Falls.

He nodded. 'Yes. I've made an arrangement with someone local that's going to keep me around the Lakes for some time, and I've been invited out to lunch to tie up a few loose ends.'

'So you're here on business?' Alexa questioned curiously, fully expecting to be told the details.

But he merely said, 'Yes. That describes it.'

'Have a nice day, then,' she said flatly, and continued to water the plants.

'I thought I might call in at the hospital to see how our young patient is getting on before I keep my appointment,' he said, eyeing her downcast face. 'How about keeping me company? I'll bring you back here afterwards.'

'Yes,' she said, immediately bouncing back. 'I was intending going myself some time during the morning, but it would be nicer if we went together.'

'Right, then,' he said. 'I'll pick you up as soon as I've had my breakfast.' Pointing himself towards the appetising smell of grilled bacon, he strolled off.

When he'd gone Alexa bounded back inside and, taking off the old jeans and sweatshirt that she'd dressed in first thing, she reached a lemon silk shirt out of the wardrobe and a pair of tight cream trousers, telling herself whimsically as she did so that she was only going hospital visiting. So why all the fuss?

While Reece had a word with the sister about the boy's condition Alexa made her way towards his bed. When he saw her coming his colour rose and she guessed that he was wishing himself anywhere but where he was. They'd been told that his name was Timothy Johnson.

Alexa said gently, 'And how are you this morning, Tim?'

He pushed himself down under the covers until only a pair of wary blue eyes were showing. 'I'm OK, thanks,' he mumbled. 'It was you that got me out of the water, wasn't it? I remember seeing you when I was lying on the bank. I nearly drowned, didn't I?'

'Yes, you did,' Reece's voice said from behind her, 'but don't keep thinking about that. Give your attention to arranging some swimming lessons. So that if there is a next time you'll be able to cope better.'

'I don't swim because I'm scared of the water,' he said uncomfortably. 'They made me go with them when I didn't want to.'

Reece patted his shoulder. 'Don't worry about it. You were very brave. I've just been talking to Sister and she says that you might be able to go home tomorrow.'

That perked him up. 'Great! I'll ask her if I can phone my mum.'

As they drove back to Craith House Alexa was silent and, after giving her a quick sideways glance, Reece said, 'You're very quiet. Are you all right?'

Her smile flashed out.

'Yes. I'm fine. I was just thinking about how different it could have been yesterday if we hadn't got to them in time, and how strange it was that we should meet under such circumstances.'

With his eyes back on the road he nodded.

'Yes, strange indeed,' he agreed sombrely, and with a sudden sinking feeling inside her Alexa thought that their meeting hadn't meant as much to him as it had to her.

Once he'd dropped her back at Craith House, Sunday became the non-event sort of day that she'd been expecting. As Alexa did her chores and helped Carol with the evening meal, she knew that she should be thankful for the respite as tomorrow there would be no time for moping.

It would be the start of another week at the practice, interesting, rewarding…and exhausting, especially at this time of year when the town was full of tourists.

There were three practice nurses—two part-timers and her-self. Annette Shaw was a thirty-five-year-old single mother with a ten-year-old daughter, and, at fast approaching sixty,

Beryl Statham, who was already a grandmother, would soon be retiring.

Of the two of them Alexa got on best with Beryl. There were huge disparities in their ages but their temperaments were the same, whereas with Annette Alexa never knew what mood she would be in.

Alexa's first task on Monday morning was to do an ESR blood test on a sixty-year-old woman suffering from poly-myalgia rheumatica. She came in to be tested once a month so that Bryan Lomas could see if the inflammation of her muscles was decreasing with the steroids that he'd pre-scribed.

The results had been good for the last six blood tests and he was reducing the medication gradually, which was a source of great pleasure to the patient as the increase in weight that the steroids had been responsible for was grad-ually disappearing.

'So, is this going to be another good result, Mrs Derby?' Alexa asked with a smile as she labelled the glass tube that she'd drawn the blood into.

'I hope so,' was the reply, 'but I've been having twinges in my forearms and I keep wondering if it's coming back.'

'Have you been involved in any unusual exercise?' she asked.

'I've been doing a lot of gardening.'

'More than usual?'

'Yes. I'd say so.'

'That could be it. Give the gardening a rest and see how you go on. Come in next Monday for the results, and then you'll know one way or the other.'

Jane Derby nodded sombrely. 'It took me ages to get clear of it the last time. Then after six months it came back. It says in my medical book that polymyalgia burns itself out in two years, but it didn't in my case.'

Alexa patted her hand consolingly. 'Don't let's cross our

bridges until we get to them. Let's see what the result is, shall we?'

She hadn't told the woman that she was fortunate that hers was a mild case that had come on gradually. Other patients with the illness had been struck down with it out of the blue and had ended up crawling on hands and knees to get help, so great had been the extent of muscle seizure. Consequently their dosages of steroids had been much higher than hers.

Beryl was already on duty in the other nurse's room, and just down the passage the three doctors were coping with the gradual procession of patients.

It was John Hendrix's last week at the practice and Alexa couldn't imagine what it was going to be like without him. It was the older man who had always found time to guide her when she'd first started and always had a sympathetic ear when she had any problems connected with the job.

She could hear his voice outside now, and the deeper tones of another man. In the next second the door opened and the elderly GP stood there. He turned and smiled at someone over his shoulder, then took a step forward and said, 'Alexa, let me introduce you to—'

'Reece Rowlinson,' she breathed. 'Er…we've already met.'

'Hello, Alexa,' the unexpected visitor said as she goggled at him in amazement. 'I deduce from your expression that I'm the last person you expected to see.'

'Yes, you are,' she said, trying to sound cool.

'Reece is going to be with the practice until the end of the year,' John Hendrix said. 'We've known each other a long time and I've persuaded him to join us for the period that he's back in England.'

He didn't enlighten the young nurse, who was popular with staff and patients alike, as to why he'd issued the invitation but, knowing the senior partner like she did,

Alexa was aware that he never did anything without a reason.

'I see,' she said slowly as surprise was replaced with pique. Turning to the man who'd scarcely been out of her mind since she'd met him, she said, 'You didn't think to let me in on the secret, then, when I was telling you what I did and where I worked?'

'Secret?' he questioned.

'I can only think that is what it was. But why? You must have known that I would find out sooner or later…as I have.'

He didn't reply, just smiled an enigmatic smile and straightened his tie, but the other man had something to say.

'I'm surprised that you know each other, but of course! You're staying at Alexa's sister's place, aren't you, Reece?'

'Yes, indeed I am,' he said easily. 'Alexa and I met on the lake—or should I say in it with regard to some of us?' Alexa glared at him but John Hendrix's thoughts were moving on, as if now the introductions were over more important matters had to be discussed.

'After today Reece will be in my room,' he said. 'I know I'm not due to finish officially until Friday, but I want to spend the rest of the week tying up loose ends and packing up my stuff. You won't have seen the last of me, you know. I'll be popping in from time to time and making a nuisance of myself.'

'You'll never be that, John,' Alexa told him fondly. 'This place won't be the same without you.'

He smiled. 'You must both come to see me some time and bring me up to date with what's going on.'

Reece was glancing over his shoulder.

'I think we need to move on, John. Alexa has someone waiting.'

'There usually is,' she said with a cool look in his direction. 'My morning is fully booked.'

John Hendrix cleared his throat. 'Point taken, Alexa. We'll leave you to it. Just as long as you understand that Reece will be in the practice as from today.'

'Yes. I understand that,' she told him.

Like many others, it was a morning of changing dressings, taking out stitches, testing blood pressure and various other duties. Before she knew it lunchtime had arrived.

'So what about the new doctor?' Beryl said while they were having a quick sandwich. 'What do you think?'

Alexa smiled. She wasn't going to tell her friend that she and Reece Rowlinson had already met. The elderly nurse was a love, but she was nosy, too, and would want to know all the ins and outs.

'I think that he's very attractive,' she said truthfully, 'but feel that he's someone who keeps his affairs close to his chest.'

Beryl was smiling. 'Are we discussing affairs of the job or the heart?'

'Affairs of the practice, of course. I can't see a man of his attractions not having affairs of the heart, but that's not our business, is it?'

'So we're only interested in finding out just how good a doctor he is?'

'Exactly.'

CHAPTER TWO

REECE *was* good. It was obvious during that first day that the newcomer to the practice was no mean performer.

Bryan Lomas and Rebecca Soames seemed to have accepted him as the third member of the team willingly enough, and if Alexa knew Bryan he would take every opportunity to unload casework onto him.

Rebecca, who was hard-working but the chilly ice-maiden type, might possibly find his presence irksome. She did the job with a sort of cold dedication, and no one as yet had been able to get to the woman beneath.

As to Alexa's own feelings about him, they were mixed. Why hadn't he told her that he was joining the practice when they'd first met and she'd told him all about herself?

Secretive in one thing…secretive in all, she thought glumly as she drove home that night. If Reece thought that now the cat was out of the bag they could talk shop when they came across each other at Craith House, he had another think coming. She saw enough of the practice during the day without bringing its problems home with her.

'Guess what?' she said to Carol when she arrived home. 'One of your guests is the new locum at the practice.'

Her sister was stirring a large pan of soup and, raising her head from the task, she eyed Alexa in surprise.

'Really! Which one? No. Let me guess. There's only one of them under sixty, so it has to be the dishy Reece Rowlinson. Am I right?'

'Yes, you are. So what do you think?'

Carol laughed.

'I think that we're very fortunate to have a doctor and a nurse on the premises.'

'I didn't mean it like that,' Alexa told her. 'I want to know what you think of him as a member of the practice.'

'Let's just say that I shall be looking forward to my next ailment.'

She had to laugh, even though she didn't feel like it. Carol wouldn't be the only female patient who now that John Hendrix was going, would be glad of an alternative to lazy Bryan Lomas, or icy Rebecca Soames. Especially when they saw that 'alternative'.

There was no sign of Reece when she went to her garden flat to change out of her uniform, but when she went to collect the evening meal that Carol provided for her, Alexa saw him seated at a table in the dining room, doing justice to the excellent food.

As she ate her own meal in the silence of her small dining kitchen her thoughts were on the weeks ahead.

All the time that she'd been hoping Reece might stay longer than the original two weeks, she'd had no idea that the man would be involved in her working life for the foreseeable future, as well as being based at Craith House.

How could she remain impersonal in that sort of set-up? But did she want to be 'impersonal'? She'd been attracted to him from the start. The only thing that was needling her was his reticence when she'd been so forthcoming about her own life.

Yet needled she was. Especially as everything about herself was an open book. She was honest and caring and had wanted to be a nurse ever since she'd been able to think for herself. Being able to work amongst the lakes once she'd qualified had been an extra bonus.

But the biggest bonus ever might be coming her way in the shape of a dark-haired doctor with inscrutable brown eyes, a jawline that said he was no pushover and the physique of the very attractive male.

And how did he see her? she wondered. That was if she impinged upon his consciousness at all. Was it as an attractive woman…or as just a minor mortal?

It had been a tiring day, but the sight of Reece Rowlinson taking an after-dinner stroll beside the lake was enough to give her a fresh lease of life. Deciding that he owed her an explanation, she set off after him.

A soft footfall behind had Reece turning from the beautiful spectacle before him. 'Ah! Florence Nightingale,' he said softly, faced with a different kind of beauty that was just as captivating.

There was no answering smile. Alexa's face was set and he remarked drily, 'Do I sense a rebuke in the offing? Only if that is the case, might I remind you that my affairs are my own concern?'

He didn't want to admit to this clear-eyed girl that on the day they'd first met he'd been having serious doubts about the arrangement he'd made with his friend John Hendrix.

Tired and out of sorts, he'd been killing time until today's introduction to the practice. Wishing he'd not got involved in another health care set-up after the gruelling months in various refugee camps. At the time Alexa had told him she was a nurse in the practice he'd still been undecided about the future.

But she'd been like a breath of clean, fresh air that day and he had to admit that knowing she was part of the staff at the lakeside practice had influenced his decision to carry out the commitment he'd made to his friend.

It would have been unethical in any case to drop out at the last moment, and he doubted whether he could have done such a thing, but the girl who was eyeing him mutinously from just a few feet away had made the decision easier. Though now the breezy friendliness that she'd shown him was missing and he didn't like it.

'May I speak now?' she asked coolly and when he nodded she went on, 'I agree that your affairs are nothing to do with me and that you may see me as a naïve person who spills out what is going on in her life to anyone who will listen. But I do think you might have told me we would be working together when I was babbling on.'

'Yes. Maybe I should have,' he said evenly. 'Although there was no offence intended. You have to remember that the last thing I was expecting you to say was that you were employed at the practice. I was completely taken aback. Especially as you were in charge of the guest house when we first met.'

'I notice that you're sidetracking and still not offering a believable explanation with regard to why you kept quiet about *your* position within the practice,' she said, with the annoyance still in her.

'No, I'm not, am I?' he agreed blandly. 'How about me taking you on the lake instead as a sign of my repentance? I believe that Craith House has a rowing boat for the use of visitors.'

It was impossible for Alexa to be angry for long and her smile flashed out. 'Yes. I'd like that…Dr Rowlinson.'

'Oh, come off it, Alexa!' he expostulated. 'My name is Reece. We don't have to be formal—we have met before.'

'All right…Reece,' she agreed meekly, and watched a smile tug at his mouth.

There was none of the lake's dark mystery tonight. The sun was still high in the sky as Reece pulled at the oars and Alexa watched him with bright curiosity.

Other rowers waved as they went past, and as one of the passenger ferries that crossed the lake at regular intervals went by, they laughed into each other's eyes as their own small craft wobbled in the wake of it.

'Do you ever go to work by boat instead of car?' Reece asked. 'I would imagine it's just as convenient.'

'Sometimes, but the car is quicker,' Alexa said absently.

Her thoughts were on other things, like the magic of the summer night, beautiful Derwentwater…and the man sitting opposite.

As she trailed her hand in the water over the side of the boat she was under his spell again, their brief exchange of words forgotten.

'How long have you lived here?' Reece asked, breaking into her thoughts.

'As long as I can remember. The big house, just down the road from my sister's place, used to belong to the Lord Mayor of Manchester and my grandfather was butler there. He brought us up, Carol and I. Our parents were killed in a power-boat accident many years ago and Grandad stepped into the breach.'

'And is he still alive?'

Alexa shook her long chestnut tresses. 'No. He died three years ago. At eighty-seven he was still very agile, but he was killed by a falling tree one day when he was helping the forestry workers.'

'Oh, that's awful! Two fatal accidents to members of your family,' he said soberly. 'What dreadful tragedies.' As the boat spun round in the wash of yet another ferry, this time going the opposite way, he added, '*I'm* going to have to take good care of *you*.'

'Yes, you'd better,' she said with an impish smile, 'or you'll have Carol to answer to.'

The sun was promising to set at last and, pointing the boat in the direction of a small marina Reece said, 'There's a bar at this place. Shall we tie up and have a drink?'

'Mmm. That would be lovely…and if it's dark when we

come out we can walk home and leave the boat here until morning. Tom won't mind coming for it. The guest house is only minutes away.'

'Whatever,' he agreed easily.

By the time they were ready to leave the marina the sky was glowing orange, with the trees on the lake edge silhouetted against it darkly, and as they walked home in the gloaming Alexa longed for him to touch her. To hold her hand, or put his arm around her shoulders. Anything would do if it made some sort of contact between them.

'What are you thinking, Alexa?' he asked softly as the village came into view. 'You're very quiet.'

'I was thinking that I haven't known you long and yet…'

'It doesn't seem like that?'

'Yes.'

Reece had stopped in mid-stride and she swallowed hard. Had he guessed what she was thinking?

It seemed as if he had, because he was reaching for her hand and drawing her towards him.

'That's the way of the world,' he murmured against the springing bronze of her hair. 'We can know someone a lifetime and never get through to the person that they really are.' His hold tightened. 'And yet someone else can walk into our lives and it's as if they've always been there.'

'So you feel the same as I do,' Alexa breathed.

He was putting her away from him gently but firmly. He knew that her mouth would be the sweetest thing he'd ever tasted if he kissed her, but the voice of reason was butting in.

He'd been on a diet of barren wastes, dirt, pain, hunger and all that went with war and famine for so long that he'd almost forgotten what it felt like to hold a beautiful woman in his arms.

And if the memory *had* been clearer it would have only brought bitterness. Thoughts of a spoilt woman from the past, who'd wanted him but not his career. Possessive and petulant when she hadn't got her own way, to the point where she had defeated her own ends and he'd gone to work in war-torn Eastern Europe, when tenderness and caring might have made him think again.

The whole affair had left a nasty taste behind, so much so that he had decided that flirtations, affairs or binding commitments weren't on his agenda. They only led to hurtful complications. He knew what it was like to be ravaged by someone else's personality and wouldn't want to wish that sort of misery onto his enchanting companion.

Alexa was watching his face change as her bright anticipation drained away. If there'd been any magic in the moment for him it had gone. He looked tired and sombre and, moving away from the shade of the trees where they'd had those sweet moments of dalliance, she began to hurry home.

'What's the rush?' Reece asked as he caught her up. 'It was a crazy moment, that's all, Alexa. Don't read anything into it.'

'As if I'm likely to!' she scoffed unsteadily. 'You're old enough to be my father.'

Laughter rumbled deep in his throat. 'Steady on! How old do you think I am?'

'I've no idea.'

'You must have. I'm thirty-five… And you…?'

'Almost twenty-six.'

'There you are, then. What's nine years between friends?'

'Friends…yes.'

He had better watch his step, Reece told himself. One second he was telling Alexa not to read anything into that tempting moment and the next he was saying that their age difference didn't matter.

It was true—it didn't. What did matter was that the life

he'd lived over recent years had made him into a loner. There were times when he thought back to what he'd seen and coped with and it made him feel tainted. While she was untouched…young, fresh and clean.

The house was in sight and Alexa had never been more glad to see it. She'd made a fool of herself and been well and truly put in her place. Reece couldn't have made it more clear that he wasn't in the market for romance when he'd told her not to read anything into those moments beneath the trees.

When they reached the gate she pushed it open quickly and called over her shoulder, 'Goodnight, Reece.'

It had been on the tip of her tongue to say, 'See you tomorrow,' but she wasn't sure that she wanted to see him the following day.

Every time their eyes met she would remember how it had felt when he'd held her close. His mouth against her hair. The clean male smell of him. The way her breasts had sprung to life at his nearness.

She would have sworn that Reece had felt the same magic, but she'd been wrong, and from now on she would tread very carefully when in the company of the latest member of the practice team.

Carol had seen her speedy farewell and Alexa had no sooner flung herself dejectedly onto the sofa than her sister was ringing the doorbell.

'What was all that about with my most dishy guest?' she asked curiously. 'Where have you been?'

'Rowing on the lake, then into the marina for a drink and after that we walked home.'

'With you legging it as if the man was after your honour,' her sister said teasingly. 'And how come you've spent the evening with him? Did he ask you to? Or did you foist yourself on him? I would be blind not to see that you're well smitten.'

'Past tense,' Alexa said mournfully, 'And, yes, Reece *did* ask me to go on the lake and afterwards to the marina. At no point did I foist myself upon him.'

Except when you followed him to the lake and were like putty in his hands, she thought guiltily.

'And so what now?' Carol wanted to know. 'Why were you in such a hurry to get away from him?'

'Because I put my foot in it as usual and he made sure that I knew it.'

'And is that all you're going to tell me?'

''Fraid so,' Alexa said dejectedly. 'You'd laugh at me if I told you the rest.'

Carol kissed her sister's smooth cheek. 'Whatever it is that's bugging you, you'll bounce back. You always do. Sleep tight, little sister. You've another busy day at the surgery ahead of you tomorrow.' And on that cheerful note she let herself out.

As the door swung to behind her Alexa groaned. That was the last thing she needed to be reminded of.

It was a warm, clear morning and because Alexa had been awake since dawn had lightened the sky she decided to walk to the practice instead of driving into Keswick.

It meant leaving earlier but that was fine. There would be no bumping into Reece as they got into their respective cars in the guest house parking area.

And by being at the practice before him, she would have a small advantage. The dedicated nurse already attending to her patients when he arrived.

As she walked across the suspension bridge that would take her out of Portinscale and onto the fields outside the busy lakeland town her bounce was back, just like Carol had said it would be.

Reece Rowlinson was someone who was just passing

through, she told herself as she walked towards the practice building. He was merely filling a gap because it suited him.

Apart from John Hendrix, no one seemed to know anything about him, including herself, and from now on if she had any sense she would stay well clear of him, unless she wanted a whole heap of heartbreak.

'So how are you getting on with Reece?' John asked when he caught her in a quiet moment in the middle of the morning.

'Fine,' Alexa told him breezily. 'He's around at both work and play.'

Tired blue eyes that didn't miss a thing were observing her. 'But of course. You'll see more of Reece than any of us if he's staying at Craith House. Did you know that he's just come back from Ethiopia? Been doctoring in refugee camps over there, and before that he was in Kosovo.'

'No, I didn't,' Alexa said in slow amazement.

Yet she wasn't really surprised. There was something special about him. A strength of purpose that would take some moving if he decided on a course of action…and he'd made it clear that his course of action with regard to a certain nurse was one of no involvement.

'No wife or family, then?' she questioned innocently.

John smiled. 'Not that I know of. But Reece has been away from these parts a long time. He was brought up in Ambleside, though his parents are long gone.

'Yet he still loves the lakes and I surmise that is why he agreed to come here for a while before he sets off on his travels again. Which means that I shall rest easy during the first few months of my retirement, knowing that two of my favourite people are holding the fort here.'

'Two?' she asked, her hazel eyes wide and questioning.

'Yes, two.' He chuckled. 'You're the other one. The best nurse we've ever had.'

Alexa felt tears prick at the affectionate vote of confidence, but she was laughing as she told him, 'As the other half of our mutual admiration society, may I say that Reece Rowlinson will find you a very hard act to follow.'

'Have no doubts on that score,' he told her. 'He's a top act himself.'

She knew that Reece had arrived. His car was parked outside the window of the nurse's room, but as yet there had been no sign of the man himself.

Until a nervous eleven-year-old girl came to have stitches removed from what had been a deep head wound sustained in a car accident.

Whether the moment was bringing back the horror of the crash or she was just strung up, Alexa didn't know, but the second she started to remove the stitches the child gave a sort of sighing groan and keeled over.

Her mother, who had been hovering, began to scream as Alexa managed to break the girl's fall with one hand, and with the other pressed the alarm button that had been installed for moments such as this.

She could see immediately that it wasn't just an ordinary faint. The child's face was blue, her lips frothy.

'What's wrong?' Reece bellowed above the screaming, as he appeared in the doorway with Bryan Lomas on his heels.

Even as he spoke he was rushing across to help her support the unconscious child and Bryan was shouting for Beryl to come to the distraught woman.

'On the couch with her!' Reece ordered urgently. 'Looks like a cardiac arrest, Alexa.'

'We're going to need an ambulance, Bryan,' he told his less agile colleague. 'Will you see to that while Alexa and I resuscitate?'

Alexa was white with disbelief. Surely a few moments of stress couldn't have brought on heart failure in an otherwise healthy child, she was thinking frantically as they worked on the unconscious girl.

There was no pulse, no heartbeat. They were in the middle of a nightmare.

At last, when she'd almost given up hope, there was success. When Alexa felt frantically at the child's slender neck there was a faint pulse and her flat little chest was moving slowly up and down. She was breathing again.

A sob of relief came up in her throat. What had just happened was what horror was made of. For a child to die while she was attending her didn't bear thinking of.

Footsteps outside in the passage announced the arrival of the ambulance crew, and as the practice staff stood by sombrely and Beryl supported the hysterical mother, the young patient was quickly transferred onto a stretcher for a fast dash to hospital.

'I'm going with her,' Reece told Bryan.

'Surely that isn't necessary,' the other man protested. 'The paramedics will cope with any further problems until they get to hospital. You'll be leaving us short-handed.'

'Nevertheless, I'm going,' he was told.

Rebecca Soames was about to make her presence felt. She'd been out on a call and had arrived at the tail end of the crisis.

'What's wrong, Bryan?' she asked in her cool, clipped voice. 'Are you fretting that you'll be late for golf?'

'Of course not,' he snapped, and turning to Reece, 'It's just that…'

He was talking to thin air. The new locum had already gone, striding swiftly after the stretcher with his arm around the shoulders of the girl's mother.

Beryl took Alexa by the arm. 'That was a nasty one,' she said. 'I'm going to make you a cup of tea. You look dreadful.'

Alexa sighed, 'I feel it. There was nothing at all to warn me that might happen.' She shuddered. 'If that poor girl had died I don't know what I would have done, and there's still a lot of cause for concern even now.'

'What about Reece the magnificent?' Beryl said with a smile that was meant to take Alexa's mind off the young patient. 'That one is nobody's pushover. Did you see how he put "Lazy Lomas" in his place?'

'Along with the help of Rebecca,' Alexa reminded her.

'Hmm. That one was positively beaming at him. Maybe the "Ice Queen" is going to thaw out at last.'

I hope not, Alexa thought dismally. For Rebecca Soames to be drawn to Reece would put the lid on a terrible day.

He was back in the early afternoon and the news he brought was mixed. The child was improving. That was the good side of it. Her life had been saved by their prompt attention.

The bad news was that she had a heart defect that no one had been aware of. She could have collapsed at any time and when tests were completed there would probably be need for surgery.

Alexa was assisting Rebecca Soames with the afternoon antenatal clinic when he got back, so their exchange of words was brief.

'Are you all right, Alexa?' he asked.

She nodded. 'Yes. I am now, but I was very fraught earlier. The thought of a child almost dying here in the surgery is something that will take some blotting out.'

'Don't even try. Problems that we put away in compartments of the mind only fester,' he said. 'I know that from experience.'

They were outside the half-open door of the nurse's room where the mothers-to-be were being attended to, and Rebecca Soames called snappily, 'Are you supposed to be assisting me or not, Nurse?'

As Alexa pushed the door back to return to her duties Reece became visible and the other woman's face lightened.

'Ah, so you're the one who's waylaying my assistant, Reece,' she said in a more pleasant tone. 'Just back from the hospital, are you?'

'Yes, Rebecca,' he said easily, 'and as afternoon surgery is about to commence I think I'd better show my face.'

She laughed as if he'd come out with some kind of witticism and Alexa's spirits sank. For the first time ever Rebecca was dropping her guard and it could only be for one reason. She fancied the new locum, which made two of them.

His concern on her own behalf seemed to have evaporated once the blonde doctor had appeared on the scene. With a dismissive nod in her direction he said, 'Let's see if we can get the rest of the day over without any more near fatalities, shall we?' And on that note he went, leaving her to wonder if he was pulling rank because Rebecca Soames was drooling over him.

One of the pregnant women who had come for her check-up was twenty-year-old Petra Purvis, who worked as a chambermaid at Craith House. She was five months into her pregnancy and blooming, with no signs of any discomfort or health problems.

Her older sister, who was also pregnant with her second child, was anything but well, with raised blood pressure and morning sickness. Today they were also going to test her for diabetes.

'I'm worried about her, Alexa,' Petra said when her sister had gone into the cubicle to undress. 'She wasn't like this when she had Chloe.'

The young nurse nodded. 'Yes. I know. But don't concern yourself too much. The high blood pressure often occurs in pregnancy, and if there is diabetes present it will disappear once the baby comes. A special diet will keep it in check for the moment.'

When she was clearing away after the clinic Alexa found herself wondering how she would feel when one day in the far distant future she was pregnant herself. But first some man would have to put a ring on her finger, after telling her how much he loved her, and at present volunteers were in short supply.

'Where's your car?' Reece asked as she was preparing to leave at the end of the day.

'I've left it at home.'

'Why?'

'Because I felt in the need of some exercise and fresh air.'

'Even though you were going to be on your feet all day?'

She sighed. 'Yes. Does it matter?'

'No. I suppose not.' He pointed to his own prestigious vehicle. 'Get in. I'll give you a lift. You've had an exhausting day.'

For some reason she didn't feel like obeying orders.

'No. Thanks just the same. I'm going to walk.'

She was being stupid and knew it. Reece was right. It had been an exhausting day.

He was observing her calmly.

'What's the matter with you? It's clear that something doesn't please you.'

Her feet were throbbing, her head aching, but she wasn't going to give in. 'I'm all right. Just leave me alone.'

'Get in the car, Alexa!' he ordered. 'You're as white as a sheet and tired. If you don't do as I say I'll pick you up and fasten you in myself.'

They were alone on the forecourt of the practice for which she was thankful. She didn't want an audience looking on when she meekly did as she was told.

Keswick was thronged with tourists as they drove

through and it wasn't until they'd left it behind on the short run to the peaceful lakeside village of Portinscale that Reece began to question his motives where Alexa Howard was concerned.

If he was looking for some light relief, she was there, obviously willing to pursue their acquaintance. But she was too sweet and vulnerable to be used in that way and after giving in to the urge to hold her close he'd disciplined himself with regard to her.

Yet he still found himself melting when she was near. He'd wanted to comfort her after the distressing incident in the surgery and would have done so if Rebecca hadn't interrupted them.

As if she was reading his thoughts, Alexa said suddenly into the silence, 'Do you realise that in the short time you've been at the practice you've achieved what no one else has been able to do?'

Reece took his eyes off the road for a second and observed her with raised brows. 'And what's that? Keep *you* in order?' he asked drily.

She eyed him unsmilingly.

'No. It's Rebecca. She's beginning to thaw out in the rays of your magical charm.'

He wanted to laugh. If there was one kind of woman that he would never be attracted to it was a cold one, but the interest that the extremely efficient woman doctor was showing in him might come in useful to save the girl at his side some heartache, should the need arise.

'Really?' he teased. 'Then I'll have to keep up the good work, won't I?'

They were at the outskirts of the village already and all the things she wanted to say to him would have to be put on hold, but Alexa did manage to get in one comment.

'You need to remember that ice can be just as dangerous

as fire,' she said with a flat profundity that had him holding back a smile.

In front of Craith House she tossed her tangled locks, opened the car door and was gone, leaving him to his thoughts.

As she deposited her bag on to the hall table a white face with tired hazel eyes looked back at her, and she thought that it was no wonder Reece had doubted her getting home under her own steam, looking as ghastly as she did.

'Had a bad day?' Carol asked when she went across for her meal.

Alexa nodded glumly. 'I was taking stitches out of a child's head wound and she suddenly collapsed with a heart attack.'

'Oh, dear!' her sister exclaimed. 'And is she all right?'

'She would have died if Reece and I hadn't worked on her. It took ages for her to come round but at last she did. Can you imagine, Caro, losing a patient in the surgery? It was a nightmare.'

'And so you and he were a team?' Carol said with a twinkle in her eye.

'Yes,' Alexa said wistfully. 'We were a team.'

'Reece Rowlinson is a name that I seem to be hearing a lot of. Does he show the same interest in you?'

'No. Not on his part.'

Carol was laughing now. 'But you're going to change all that.'

'That'll be the day!' Alexa hooted. 'That man puts me in my place better than anyone I know.' Her face softened. 'We're lucky to have him at the practice, though. He's way out of our league. Reece works abroad most of the time, wherever the need is greatest in under-developed countries. The six months he's spending with us is just a break from it. Then he'll be going back.'

Carol was frowning. 'All the more reason for you not to get too involved.'

'Yes, I know, but...'

'You're going to be?'

'What?' she questioned absently as the memory of being held in his arms came back.

'Involved!' Carol said reproachfully.

For the rest of the week it was business as usual at the practice, with regular patients and a smattering of visitors seeking the services of the staff.

There was always a large percentage of falls amongst visitors who came into the surgery and Alexa often wondered if it was because the public were less careful when on holiday. Maybe they expected to lead a charmed life while away, and it was not the case.

On the Friday morning she'd already had Mark Mitchell, a young boy with a badly cut knee, passed on to her from Reece, and from Bryan an elderly man who'd fallen, almost on the doorstep of the practice. *He* was going to have to go to Accident and Emergency.

While waiting for the ambulance to arrive, Alexa bathed Mark's knee, which was bleeding badly.

Beryl was making a cup of hot sweet tea for the old man who was very shocked.

'There's a possibility of a fractured wrist here, Nurse,' Bryan had said when he'd brought him to their room. 'He needs to be X-rayed and as he's in no fit state to make his own way to the hospital, the ambulance is coming here for him.'

When Reece found out some minutes later he told her, 'They might as well take young Mark, too. It's a deep cut and he's going to need stitches. Be sure to inform the paramedics that I've given him a tetanus jab.'

He was eyeing the sniffling youngster. 'Who's he with?'

'No one at the moment,' she told him. 'He was on his skateboard and had a spill. We've phoned for his mother to come to the surgery.'

'And what if he's already gone to the hospital by the time she gets here? You'd better call her again and tell her to go straight there instead of coming here first,' he said with a sort of brisk impatience that made her feel there was implied reproof in his manner.

He'd been keeping himself at a distance ever since the night that he'd driven her home, which was more than she could say for his attitude towards Rebecca, and after what he'd just said her resentment boiled over.

'When I rang his mother I wasn't aware that you were sending him to hospital,' she said coolly. 'That is a decision you've only just made, and as I'm not a mind-reader, certainly not when it comes to yours, I wasn't able to pass on that information to her. But I will do it now.'

'Fine,' he said blandly, and now he was smiling. But the beam was going over her head and when she turned Alexa found Rebecca behind her.

CHAPTER THREE

ON SATURDAY mornings the surgery was open from nine o'clock to ten for emergencies or for the collecting of prescriptions that had been requested.

There was always just one doctor present and a nurse. Alexa, Annette and Beryl did it on a rota basis, and this week it was Annette's turn, leaving the other two nurses free to do whatever they had planned for the weekend.

If she wasn't working Alexa always helped Carol with departures and arrivals at the guest house, and this Saturday was no different.

'Dr Rowlinson has extended his stay with us for a while longer,' her sister said as they busied themselves behind the reception desk.

Alexa's face brightened. At least that meant that he would still be around Craith House in the evenings and at weekends. It was good news, even though she was supposed to be staying clear of Reece as much as possible.

What was he planning for the rest of his stay? she wondered. Would he keep extending his time with them, or find himself some other kind of temporary accommodation?

No doubt he had it all planned if what she'd seen of him so far was an indication of the type of man he was. Yet he didn't seem in any hurry to leave Craith House.

Amongst the new arrivals that morning were two walkers, sturdy, tanned young men in their twenties, and as Alexa booked them in, with her mind still on Reece, she was unaware of their appreciative glances.

It didn't go unnoticed by someone else, though. Reece

was making his way through the reception area on his way out, and as the porter picked up their luggage and began to lead the way up the staircase he said in a low voice, 'You'll have some kindred spirits in those two.'

'Huh!' she scorned. 'I'm not into trudging about in boots...or mixing with kids.'

'Kids! They're the same age as yourself.'

'Are you trying to tell me something?'

'I might be.'

'Such as, stay with my own age group? Is that why you've been so snappy with me ever since you gave me a lift home the other night?'

'I haven't been "snappy", as you describe it. I'm merely thinking of your welfare.'

'And supposing I think that my welfare would be best served by being in your company, what then? Or is all this because you've become very chummy with Dr Soames?'

'You're letting your imagination run riot, Alexa, in more ways than one. But I must be off. I'm having lunch with John today.'

'Lucky you,' she said wistfully. 'John is one of my favourite people. I shall miss him.'

'Yes, I'm sure you will, but he'll still be around, don't forget. He won't be disappearing like me when my six months are up.'

He's doing it again, she thought, warning her off. Dropping hints that he was just passing through. Well, she could take a hint.

'Have a nice day,' she said flatly, ignoring the opening for discussion that he'd dangled in front of her.

A taxi was depositing the next lot of new arrivals at the gate and with a quick look at her set face he went.

Reece hadn't told her that when he and the elderly GP had been arranging to have lunch together John had said casually, 'Bring Alexa with you if she's free, Reece. She's like a ray of light in the darkness of my old age.'

But she hadn't been free, had she? She'd been helping out at the guest house, so he'd had an excuse for not passing on the invitation.

A bit mean perhaps, but he knew without being told that Alexa would have managed to make it somehow, and it would only have meant watching his step again, avoiding her candid hazel gaze and being generally aloof. When what he really wanted to do was hold her close again and let the magic take over.

As Reece drove to John's house in the village of Grasmere he was remembering her lack of interest in the two walkers. *They* were the kind of people she should be making friends with, not a disillusioned-with-the-world-in-general doctor.

A smile tugged at his mouth as he remembered how she'd said he was old enough to be her father. She'd been upset because he wasn't prepared to succumb to the attraction between them, and he'd wanted to strike back by telling her that there was nothing fatherly in his feelings for her. But what would that have led to? A passionate affair that would have to be cut short if he kept to his arrangements. He'd been down that road before and once was enough.

An echo from the past came back, a shrill voice telling him to choose. And he had chosen, and so far he'd never regretted his decision.

As always at weekends in the holiday season, Grasmere was busy, with tourists wandering round the old church and its graveyard and browsing in the craft shops.

This place and Ambleside, with their own particular charm, were the two places that he'd held in his heart all his life, and coming back to Cumbria for this short time he'd hoped to find peace.

* * *

'And so what do you think of the practice from what you've seen so far?' John asked Reece as they sat in the garden of the old house where he'd lived for most of his life.

Like most of the houses in Grasmere, it was built of Cumberland slate, with all the varying colours and thicknesses combining to make them dwellings of distinction.

The elderly GP had lost his wife some years previously and his son and daughter were both living abroad, which meant that he was going to have time on his hands.

If it hadn't been for the ill health that had plagued him in recent months he would still have been working, holding the reins in his capable hands.

But the onset of prostate cancer and a heart that wasn't as good as it used to be had forced him to make the decision that he would have dearly have liked to have put off.

He was waiting for an answer to his question and Reece was debating what to say. Obviously John would want the truth, but to give it to him in a way that wouldn't distress him wasn't going to be easy. Diplomacy was called for.

'Bryan seems a decent enough doctor, but he will never come up to your standards,' was his opening remark. 'He seems to lack drive.'

'Aye, he does,' the older man agreed, 'but only in the surgery. There's nothing feeble about him on the golf course.'

'I see.'

Rebecca's comment when Bryan had been fussing about him leaving the surgery to accompany the heart-attack child and her mother to hospital had been about 'missing his golf'.

He'd better not come with any of those sort of tricks while he was around, or, locum or not, he would pass on a few home truths. A doctor who was less than totally committed was no use to anyone.

Thinking of Rebecca, what could he say about her? She

was good. No doubt about that. But she needed a personality transplant. Or maybe that was a bit steep. It was comparing her with Alexa that made the blonde doctor seem so
unattractive. But, then, everyone would seem pale beside
Alexa.

'And Rebecca?' John was asking.

'She's fine. A very good doctor. Rather reserved, but that
is her own affair.'

The other man nodded. 'My sentiments exactly. And the
nurses? Alexa Howard, for instance?'

'Ideal for the job,' he said sincerely. 'Efficient, capable,
extremely hard working, yet with a bubbly sort of charm
that's very endearing.'

John was staring at him in surprise. 'Well! You've certainly got that one sorted.'

Reece laughed. 'Don't forget that I'm in her company
morning, noon and night.'

'Aye. I forgot that you're staying at her sister's place.'

'Alexa and I met under rather unusual circumstances,'
he informed his friend. 'We didn't have time to be introduced. She was covered in algae and I was wobbling about
beside her in a rowing boat, about to heave an unconscious
youngster on board.'

'Sounds interesting.'

'It was—very.'

He wasn't going to tell John that he'd been losing his
sense of direction ever since that occasion.

'You're not planning on staying at Craith House all the
while you're here, are you?' the other man was asking.
'Shouldn't you be looking for somewhere less restricting?'

'I suppose so.'

It would be the sensible thing to do, but all he would
see of Alexa then would in their respective positions at the
surgery.

'Lunch is ready,' a voice said from behind them, and

both men turned to see Elizabeth Maddox, John's house-keeper, beckoning from the French windows.

A pleasant, middle-aged woman, with dark hair in a styl-ish cut and serene brown eyes, she had been with him ever since his wife had died. As the three of them sat down to eat, John amazed Reece by saying, 'Elizabeth and I have something to tell you. I've asked her to marry me...and she's said yes.'

'That's wonderful news!' he cried, and it was.

Liz, as John fondly called her, would be there for him whatever the circumstances, but it would make all the dif-ference for John to have her with him as his wife.

'The wedding is next Saturday,' he said, to Reece's fur-ther surprise. 'It will be just a quiet affair as both of my kids are far away and Liz's parents are dead. But I'd like you to be there, Reece, *and* the staff from the practice. Will you pass the word round? Two o'clock at the church here, and then a reception at the Old Swan Hotel.'

When Reece went down for his dinner that evening Alexa was waitressing in the dining room, and as she took his order for a starter he said, 'I'm the bearer of good tidings.'

She paused briefly. 'Such as?'

'You're invited to a wedding.'

'Not Rebecca Soames and yourself, I hope.'

'You're a cheeky lady,' he said, trying not to smile. 'I shall have to have a word with your sister about the way you talk to her guests.'

'Guest.'

'Huh?'

'You're the only one I talk to like that.'

She glanced around her quickly. 'Are you going to tell me who's getting married or not? Carol has put the soup out and it will be going cold.'

'John is marrying his housekeeper on Saturday next and everyone from the practice is invited.'

Alexa's face lit up. 'John is going to marry the lovely Liz!' she exclaimed. 'That's wonderful news!' There was a pause and he could almost hear the wheels turning. 'I don't suppose they're looking for a bridesmaid?'

'I doubt it,' he said drily. 'Or a pageboy for that matter.'

Carol was eyeing her from the doorway and Alexa got the message. 'I'll talk to you later,' she said quickly, and as Reece nodded she moved smartly towards the kitchen.

'I'm going to a wedding next Saturday,' she told Carol as they cleared away after the meal.

Her sister paused in the middle of stacking the dishwasher. 'Whose, for heaven's sake?'

'John's.'

'Really? Who's he marrying?'

'His housekeeper.'

'Well! That's a turn up for the book. What will you wear?'

'Something peach, I think. It's a colour that suits me.'

Carol was observing her thoughtfully. 'I suppose Reece will be there, him being a friend of John's.'

'Of course.' Alexa beamed. 'And all the rest of the staff, too.'

'How nice of the old man to invite you all.'

'Mmm,' she murmured. 'It's so sad that it's John who's going. If it had been Bryan or Rebecca I wouldn't have minded. But John was the best doctor I've ever worked with.'

'Was? Past tense?'

'Well, yes. He's leaving, isn't he? And I have to admit that his temporary replacement is the only one I've ever met who is as good as John.'

Carol was laughing. 'How did I know you were going to say that?'

Alexa groaned. 'Am I so predictable?'

''Fraid so,' her sister said in continuing amusement, and continued on a more serious note, 'So, have you got a little number in the wardrobe? Or are we going to have to do a quick dash round the boutiques?'

'I don't know. What do you think? I *have* got a couple of nice outfits I could wear. But not in peach. One blue and the other pale green. I think I'll buy something new.'

'So when do we shop?'

'That's just it. I don't know. Unless I take a half-day's leave. I'm working all week and can't risk leaving it until next Saturday morning with the wedding that afternoon.'

'Do that, then,' Carol suggested. 'And I'll make sure that I'm free from here for a couple of hours. Tom will hold the fort.

'I don't suppose this desire to buy something new has anything to do with a certain locum on the loose, has it?' she continued in a teasing voice. 'That is presuming Reece Rowlinson isn't already spoken for.'

Alexa was looking at her aghast. 'I never thought of that.'

'Surely you realise that there aren't many men of his age group who haven't had some kind of long-term relationship. Very often there is someone in the background.'

'You mean ex-wives and children?'

'Or even present wives.'

'Oh, Carol! Do you think so?'

Her sister shook her head. 'No. I'm merely pointing out that he is very attractive and someone, somewhere along the way, might have taken note of that.'

*   *   *

It had been a casual conversation but it put the blight on the rest of the weekend, and all day Sunday Alexa moped around her garden flat with her spirits at a low ebb.

Being the kind of person she was, it was hard not to go and knock on the door of room number five in the guest house and ask Reece if he did have any 'baggage'.

But, having a pretty good idea of the kind of reception the question would get, she refrained. In any case, Reece wouldn't have been there if she *had* gone to see him.

He'd left early that morning to go walking with Greg and Dave, the two fellows she'd scorned to accept as more her type of person than he was.

'I'll do the veg,' she told Carol in the late afternoon as the preparations for Sunday's evening meal got under way.

'Do I detect that someone is at a loose end?' Tom asked when she made the offer. 'You should have gone with your doctor friend and the other two guys.'

'Huh!' she snorted with a toss of her head. 'There's such a thing as being asked.'

'Yes, I suppose so,' her brother-in-law agreed absently. He placed a huge pile of carrots and turnips fresh from the garden in front of her. 'You can start on these, Alexa, while I go and gather some green beans.'

When it was time for dinner to be served the three men hadn't returned and Alexa asked Carol, 'Where were they intending going, Caro?'

'Tom says he heard them mention Scafell, and there has been heavy rain all afternoon, don't forget. That will have slowed them down.'

When it got to nine o'clock and there was still no sign of them, Alexa became anxious. Scafell was a tough climb at the best of times and she always felt that the mountain had a forbidding look about it.

Supposing that they'd lost their way in the driving rain. That mists had come down and… They would have to call

Mountain Rescue if they didn't show up soon, she thought worriedly.

Another half-hour went by and when Reece came strolling into reception at a quarter to ten Alexa went weak with relief.

He looked tired and grimy and when he saw her face he said, 'I'm sorry if we've caused any anxiety. Dave fell and fractured his ankle. It took ages to get him down off the mountain and to hospital.

'It's a bad break so they're going to keep him in for a couple of days. Greg will be arriving shortly. I came on ahead as I thought that you might be alarmed when we didn't appear for dinner.'

'No, not really,' she told him perversely, having no wish to let him see that she'd been anxious and on edge. 'It happens all the time, guests deciding to eat somewhere else if they can't get back in time.'

He sighed and she hoped that he was disappointed by her response. Or maybe the sigh was for the meal he'd missed, as his next remark was, 'Can you rustle up some food? I'm starving.'

'Yes, of course, Dr Rowlinson,' Carol said from behind her. 'Your table is still set in the dining room. We have soup on offer, cold meat, salad and a sweet. If that's all right, Alexa will see to you.'

His grimy face broke into a smile and it wasn't directed at her, Alexa thought. Carol was its recipient, for the very good reason that she was offering sustenance. No doubt Reece was thinking that it was a good job that somebody cared, after the cool reception he'd received from herself.

By the time the food was ready Greg had arrived back from the hospital, and after they'd washed and changed the two late arrivals presented themselves in the dining room.

They ate with relish and had little to say to the young waitress until their hunger had abated, although Alexa was aware of Reece's eyes upon her as she went to and from the kitchen.

He would choke on his raspberry roulade if he knew what was on her mind, she thought glumly, but it was hardly the moment to ask if he'd picked up any attachments in recent years, such as a wife and children.

The words 'nosy', 'interfering' and 'intrusive' came to mind. No doubt he would come out with all of those were she to pose the question, but sooner or later she would have to ask.

'Thanks for that, Alexa,' he said at last. 'I can't remember when last I enjoyed a meal so much. I was famished, and now I'm going to turn in, or I shall be at less than my best tomorrow at the practice.' Leaving her feeling miserable and frustrated, he departed.

Jane Derby was anxious to find out the results of the ESR blood test, which would tell her if the polymyalgia had come back, and Alexa could understand why. She was dreading having to go back on the steroids.

On Monday morning she was the first patient to be seen by a doctor, and when Alexa saw her coming out of Bryan's consulting room there was a smile on her face.

'I'm all right, Nurse.' She beamed. 'It hasn't come back. It must have been all the gardening I've been doing that made me think it had. I can't tell you how thankful I am. I've been praying I wouldn't have to go back on the medication. Dr Lomas says that the inflammation level in my muscles is still down. I'll need monthly checks, but it looks as if it might have gone for good.'

Alexa smiled. 'I'm pleased for you, Mrs Derby. That's really good news.' As the woman went happily on her way the young nurse wished that the woman waiting in her treatment room had as much to smile about.

Frances Conroy had been given laser surgery for an intestinal complaint, and somewhere along the way she'd picked up an infection, resulting in an open wound that needed to be dressed each day until it had cleared.

Normally a strong-minded, sensible thirty-plus, the present situation was really upsetting her and every time she came to have the dressing changed Alexa was faced with her distress.

'The infection is clearing, Frances,' she'd told her only that morning. 'I know that it's been slow and very worrying for you, but it's all going to come right in the end. You'll see.'

'I hope you're right, Nurse,' Frances had said dismally. 'I know that the operation turned out to be more complicated than expected, but I never thought I'd have to put up with this afterwards.'

Reece's car had still been outside Craith House when she'd left that morning, and Alexa had wondered if he'd overslept after the previous day's exertions. But the queue outside his consulting room was slowly decreasing, so obviously he had arrived. After all, she thought with a wry smile, he didn't have to report to her every time he appeared.

'And so what was all that about yesterday?' he asked as he brought her the notes for a patient he was passing on to her.

'I'm not with you,' she said with assumed perplexity.

'Oh, no? I'm talking about your lack of concern when we got back after a disastrous day.'

'I'm not public relations officer at Craith House, you know. I do have my own life to live. I merely help out whenever possible,' she said calmly, grateful that he hadn't seen the state she'd been in before his arrival.

If he had done, it would have made Reece even more wary of letting her into his life. Yet wasn't he doing the exact opposite by showing her that he was upset at her lack of concern?

'I see. Or do I?' he said levelly. Then his voice softened. 'I don't want us always to be at cross purposes, Alexa. We're living and working in close proximity and I'd like us to find a level that we can cope with...for your sake more than mine.'

'And what sort of a level do you have in mind?' she asked in a tight whisper, aware that other members of staff were in the vicinity. 'Ever since you held me close that night when we'd been on the lake, you've kept your distance.'

He sighed. 'I have my reasons.'

'Could one of them be that you're choosy?'

'Hardly. *You* are in a class of your own.'

She ignored that comment and went on in the same angry whisper, 'Or is it because you've got your life all nicely mapped out? And with regard to that, is there a problem because you've got a wife and family tucked away somewhere?'

If she hadn't been so aghast at the way she'd put the question Alexa might have seen the amused surprise in his eyes, but all she could do was look down at the carpet like some wayward child about to be chastised.

'This is hardly the place to be discussing such matters, is it?' he said drily. 'I always take a walk beside your lake after dinner. If you want an answer, come and join me.'

'*My* lake?' she questioned, avoiding the issue.

'Yes. Derwentwater is your lake, isn't it? You've been brought up beside it. Just as Grasmere is John's favourite, and mine the vast waters of Windermere that embrace Ambleside. And so?'

'What?'

'I'll see you tonight.'

'Yes, I suppose so.'

She would be there. But if the man who was striding back into his consulting room did have something to hide she would want to curl up and die.

For the rest of the day Alexa dealt with the never-ending procession of those requiring her attention, with Beryl to help her in the morning and Annette in the afternoon.

It was as she was giving an elderly woman a B_{12} injection for the anaemia which had manifested itself with a constant tingling of the hands that Rebecca appeared in the doorway and announced, 'Reece and I are leaving early, Nurse. We're going to choose a wedding present for Dr Hendrix.'

Alexa observed her with surprised hazel eyes. First, because there was a gratified smile on the face that was usually expressionless and, second, because as far as she knew there had been no collection.

The rest of the staff had only found out today about the retiring partner's imminent wedding and there had been much surprise but little action…until now.

'But we haven't collected yet!' she exclaimed.

'I'm aware of that,' Rebecca said with a sigh. 'The gift that Reece and I are going to purchase is from the partners. The rest of you can do as you wish.'

'I see,' Alexa said blandly. 'We will. Thanks for letting us know.'

Rebecca smiled again and Alexa thought that it couldn't be true. The mask of ice cold Dr Soames had cracked twice in one day.

She was ready for off when the two doctors came back, and with a casual wave she drove past them as they pulled up in front of the surgery.

A glimpse of Rebecca's expression made her think that the thaw hadn't lasted long. The blonde doctor looked much less chirpy than she had earlier.

As she left the town behind Alexa thought that whatever

they'd bought for John, she had some ideas of her own with regard to the rest of the staff, and no one would be able to say they weren't original.

A home brewing kit was one. A kilt, as he'd always claimed to have Scottish ancestry, was another, and a cocker spaniel puppy was something else she'd thought of. Only the other day the elderly GP had been saying that now he was retiring he would like a dog, a spaniel for preference.

It was half past eight when she saw Reece make his way towards the lakeside. Throwing a cardigan over the sleeveless cotton top and trousers that she'd changed into, Alexa followed him.

She felt like a stalker, but the offer had been there to meet him and she couldn't refuse. If she ended up going back with the bounce taken out of her she would have only herself to blame for nosying into Reece's private life.

'Ah! Alexa!' he said coolly. He pointed to a fallen log by the water's edge. 'Take a seat.'

She eyed him warily. 'If you're going to start making fun of me, I'm going.'

'Without hearing the answer to your question? I think I know you better than that.'

'You don't know me at all,' she countered snappily. 'Not the woman underneath.'

He was observing her with a sort of amused gravity that made her want to rush up to him and bang her fists against his chest, but if ever there was a moment for dignity, this was it.

As if he thought he'd kept her waiting long enough, Reece became serious. 'I don't know why I'm telling you this, Alexa,' he began, 'because it's none of your business, but as you're so curious, I'll oblige.

'I am not and never have been married. Not because the

idea doesn't appeal to me, but because for some years I've been employed in situations where I would not want to take a wife, and yet neither would I have wanted to leave one behind. And I have to tell you that it's a situation that isn't likely to change in the foreseeable future. Does that answer your question?'

She swallowed hard. The good news that he carried no baggage had been blotted out by the last part of what he'd had to say, and something about the way he'd said it told her that he wasn't intending changing his mind.

But could *she* change it for him? Yes! She could! Moving closer she put her arms around him and with her face against his collar she said softly, 'But what about us, Reece? Are you going to turn your back on me?'

He groaned, raising his eyes heavenwards as he did so.

'There's nothing to turn my back on, Alexa. I wouldn't wish my lifestyle onto any woman. And as for you, you're too vibrant and beautiful to get embroiled in it.'

Her lips were only inches away from his as she breathed, 'Why don't you let me be the judge of that, Reece?'

With an effort of will that brought him out in a sweat, he said, 'You're too pushy, Alexa. I prefer to do my own hunting.'

That did it. She wrenched herself out of his arms as if he had something catching and with a sob in her throat she cried, 'Well, thanks for that! You don't see anything wrong in Rebecca drooling over you, but when it comes to me...I'm pushy. You can rest assured that I won't be "pushing" any more. From now on, as far as I'm concerned, that's it!'

As Alexa marched back the way she'd come, Reece didn't move. He knew if he did he would find himself chasing after her and telling her all the things she wanted to hear as he took her in his arms.

Being in her company again after an irritating afternoon

with Rebecca Soames had been like wine after water, but he'd had to say what he had.

The last thing he wanted was for Alexa to get the wrong idea about where their relationship was heading. Yet why? There was already a bond between them. The attraction had been there from the moment of meeting. It was only to be expected that she saw a future for them.

He knew that he was using the job as an excuse not to respond to her, when all the time it was a secondary thing. It was what had happened between Natalie and himself that was the real reason why he chose to walk a solitary road.

The hurt of it remained. His pride had been in shreds, his disillusionment complete. But was it right that Alexa should be made to suffer because of that?

He'd been taken aback at her wanting to know if he was married. If she'd known him better she wouldn't have needed to ask.

And now he'd made an even worse mess of things by telling her she was pushy. What a choice of words! She was the most delightful thing he'd ever seen but he was keeping her at arm's length like some nervous schoolboy and had insulted her in the bargain.

The last thing he'd expected when he'd agreed to join a practice beside Derwentwater had been to find a nurse there who had cast a spell on him within minutes of their meeting.

CHAPTER FOUR

WHEN Reece got back to the guest house Carol had a message for him.

'John Hendrix phoned while you were out,' she said with a smile for the most mesmeric visitor they'd ever had at Craith House. 'He asks if you'll ring him, please.'

He nodded with an answering smile and wondered if he should have a word with Carol about how he didn't want to hurt her younger sister. But caution told him it wouldn't be wise. If Alexa found out she would be even more angry than she was already.

And in any case, what would he say to Carol? That he found Alexa riveting…rebellious…sweet…and funny? That he was sorely tempted to pursue their relationship, but it wouldn't be fair?

It was a wonder that the boot wasn't on the other foot, with Carol having something to say to him, along the lines of his seniority in almost everything compared to Alexa's beguiling, youthful impetuosity.

He wouldn't be able to blame Carol if she did take him to task, but she hadn't done so as yet, which made him think that maybe Alexa hadn't told her about the attraction between them.

There was no sign of Alexa but, then, he hadn't expected there to be. Her curtains were drawn and there was a stillness about the garden flat that couldn't be misinterpreted. It said that its occupant was not available.

The thought brought a twist to his mouth. It was the opposite to that state of affairs that he'd described earlier. He'd said she was pushy rather than too available, but the inference had been there, and now he had a sinking feeling that she'd gone to ground.

Thank God they worked in the same place. If she was going to be hiding herself away here at Craith House, at least he would be able to see her at the practice.

And if ever there was an example of contradictory thinking that was it, he told himself as he went to call his friend. One minute he was giving Alexa her marching orders, and the next he was clinging to the fact that they wouldn't be totally out of touch.

'Liz has been scolding me because I omitted to ask you to be my best man on Saturday,' John said when he answered the phone. 'It was one of the reasons I asked you to lunch, to ask the favour of you, and when you'd gone she couldn't believe that I'd forgotten. Will you do it, Reece?'

'Yes, of course,' he said immediately. 'I'd be honoured. Are we dressing up? Morning suits and the rest?'

The other man chuckled. 'No. Nothing like that. I'm too long in the tooth for that kind of thing. Just an ordinary suit will do. Liz's uncle is giving her away. She'll be wearing a long frock and a big hat.'

'Right,' Reece said absently, as a vision of someone else in bridal attire came to mind. Alexa in ivory brocade that clung to her slender curves and made the long mane of her hair stand out in glowing bronze…with a floating veil that was lifting in the breeze…and…

'Are you still there, old chap?' John was asking.

'Er…yes…of course,' he said hurriedly as the bemusing picture faded. 'I'll see you on Saturday, then.'

'You look really elegant,' Carol said when Alexa presented herself for inspection on the afternoon of the wedding. 'You were right about the peach. It brings out the lights in your hair and makes your eyes look like warm brown velvet.'

Alexa managed a smile, and there hadn't been many of those around during the past week. But if there were no accolades forthcoming from anyone else, at least she could rely on Carol.

Her manner towards Reece during the last few days had been coldly polite. On one occasion when she'd been unsure of what he wanted her to do regarding a patient and she'd presented herself in his consulting room with an expression that would have made Rebecca's seem positively radiant, he'd said exasperatedly, 'For goodness' sake, Alexa. Can't we at least be friends?'

'No,' she'd said flatly, and continued before he could comment, 'Do you want me to put a fresh dressing on little Tiffany's burn, or leave it to heal without? I usually make those kind of decisions myself, but as you saw her before she came to me I thought I'd better make sure, as I don't want to be guilty of any other transgressions.'

He'd sighed. 'Now you're being ridiculous. Another dressing, I think.'

As she'd marched back to her own domain Alexa had thought grimly that, ridiculous she may be, at least she knew her own mind, especially where he was concerned.

But that minor incident was now in the past. It was the day of Dr John's wedding and she was content to know that she was looking her best in a peach silk dress and three-quarter-length matching coat, offset by a wide-brimmed straw hat and matching shoes.

And if a certain person still kept his distance when he saw her so attired...she would go and jump in the lake.

Which would only make him more certain that she wasn't the one for him, she told herself as she put the finishing touches to her make-up and prepared to sally forth.

The partners, excluding Reece, who had expressed a wish to buy his own gift for the bridegroom, had bought John Hendrix a Teasmade and a set of antique stone hot-water bottles, which had caused much mirth amongst the rest of the practice.

'I don't know why they didn't buy him a year's supply of denture cleaner,' Beryl had said with a smile. 'It would be just as original as that lot.'

'Probably because John doesn't wear dentures,' Annette had pointed out, and there had been laughter in the nurse's room.

The rest of them had agreed with Alexa's suggestion for their own gift, and a delightful cocker spaniel puppy had been delivered to the house in Grasmere the previous evening.

If they'd had any doubts about their choice, the look on the elderly doctor's face when he'd seen it had quickly dispelled them.

What Reece was giving his friend she didn't know, but Alexa expected him to have used more imagination than Rebecca and co. Even though it was in short supply when it came to herself.

Although the sun was beating down outside, it was cool and shadowed inside the old church as Reece deposited himself next to John in the first pew.

For some reason Wordsworth's famous words came into his mind. Probably because he was amongst the places that the poet had known and loved.

'I wandered lonely as a cloud…'

I'm lonely, Reece thought, and who, or what, is to blame for that?

The kind of work he did *was* partly responsible, but he'd already admitted it wasn't just that. Betrayal had left a bitter taste and it was still there.

He could have been married a dozen times, but after

Natalie he'd made sure he never stopped in one place long enough to give the matter the consideration it deserved.

Yet as a pair of mutinous hazel eyes came to mind he admitted that he could get dangerously close to the idea if he wasn't careful.

Footsteps were sounding on the stone floor behind him. The church was filling up. John was too well known in the area for his wedding to be the quiet affair he desired.

Taking a quick look over his shoulder, Reece saw Alexa walking down the aisle with Beryl. His eyes widened. She looked cool and elegant in the peach silk outfit.

The unruly mass of her hair was swept back into stylish coils on the back of her head and perched on top was a hat of the palest of peach straw.

He could feel his heart pounding. If she was out to make a point she was succeeding. He was totally mesmerised by her.

'You've got the ring, I hope?' John said at that moment, and Reece was brought back to the occasion and his duties regarding it.

He smiled. 'Yes, I have, and if we'd forgotten it I could be there and back from your place in two ticks.'

'Show me?'

Putting his hand in his waistcoat pocket, Reece brought forth the heavy gold band and the other man was satisfied.

Reece was eyeing him fondly. He owed this man a lot. He'd lost his parents when only in his teens and been devastated, but John had been there for him. He'd been the family doctor in those days and he'd taken him under his wing, to the extent of having Reece live with him until he'd gone off to medical college.

John's wife had been alive then and she had been just as kind to him, and now the man who'd been like a father to him was about to be married again, to someone who would love and cherish him just as she had.

His chest felt tight and Reece told himself that he was getting maudlin. Was it the sight of Alexa in all her youthful allure that was getting to him? Making him realise what he might be passing by because he'd set himself a path with no turnings?

The organist had been playing quietly but now the instrument pealed forth with the familiar strains of the wedding march. The serene Liz, dressed in the palest of blues, was walking sedately towards them on the arm of a very elderly uncle, followed by her sister in a suitable outfit of delicate pink.

Alexa's glance had been on Reece from the moment of entering the church, and when he'd turned briefly she'd hoped for some sort of acknowledgement. But his appraisal of what was going on behind him had been a fleeting thing and communication with anyone, least of all herself, seemed to be the last thing on his mind.

As the elderly bridegroom and his bride made their vows, with none of the hesitancy of the young and inexperienced, Alexa felt tears prick, yet she didn't know why.

She wasn't the type to weep easily. In nursing one got used to keeping a hold on the emotions, but there was something about the brief yet binding ceremony taking place before them that was making her tearful.

The last thing she would want Reece to see when the ceremony was over was 'Miss Pushy' in tears, so with a few quick snuffles into a scrap of lace she forced them back.

'We're allowed to shed a few tears at weddings, you know,' Beryl said in a low voice as the wedding party went into the vestry to sign the register.

Alexa managed a watery smile. 'Why is that, do you think?'

'Lots of reasons,' the older woman said solemnly. 'Such as it bringing back fond memories of one's own wedding. Or the reciting of the vows and the atmosphere in church.'

She went on with a teasing smile, 'And there are those who might have yearnings towards the best man that are not being reciprocated fast enough.'

Alexa groaned. 'You've got it in one, Beryl. How did you guess?'

'You're an open book, Alexa. Go for it, *if* the new locum is what you want.'

At that moment the organ struck up again in a less sedate manner than at the beginning of the service, and as John and Liz came down the aisle to its joyful strains, with the best man and the solitary bridesmaid close behind, Reece's glance met hers and Alexa's world righted itself.

'I hardly recognised you,' he said with a quirky smile as they stood in the lounge of the hotel where the reception was being held.

A waiter was hovering and as they helped themselves to sherry Reece lowered his voice. 'You are a vision to behold.'

Alexa gave him a quick sideways glance.

'Is that what you really think?'

The smile had gone and now the look on his face was almost as if he were in pain.

'Yes. You are the most attractive woman in the room, Alexa, and not just because of what you're wearing. When I said that I hardly recognised you, it was because so far I've only seen you in your nurse's uniform or in casual clothes.'

She smiled up at him with joy inside her. However much it was costing him, and from his expression it was quite a bit, Reece was telling her that she was beautiful.

'So you're seeing me in a different light?' she teased.

'Not necessarily.'

'I'm still seen as the vestal virgin who has to be protected from life's quagmires, am I?'

'Yes, if that is what you are, and if you don't stop teasing I might be tempted to do something to rectify that state of affairs.'

He watched her colour rise in a hot tide and knew that he was throwing caution to the winds after all his vows to do the opposite. She had that effect on him.

Before Alexa had the chance to answer back the guests were asked to take their places at the tables. As Reece took his seat beside the bride and groom, she went to sit with Beryl who had been watching their exchange of words from a distance.

'And so what has brought the colour to your peaches-and-cream complexion?' she asked.

Alexa shrugged. 'Just Reece Rowlinson making promises that he has no intentions of keeping.'

'You are sorry to say?'

'Maybe. Maybe not,' she said wistfully as the man in question got to his feet to make a speech.

It was like everything else he did—witty, sincere and efficiently accomplished. As Alexa joined in the applause her spirits lifted.

They hadn't known each other long. Eventually Reece would see that she was the one for him and then...

John and his bride had gone and the rest of the practice staff were drifting off towards their own pursuits for a summer evening when Reece appeared beside her again.

'I need your advice,' he said in a low voice.

'You need my advice!' Alexa said in exaggerated surprise.

'Yes. Where are you going from here?'

'Back to Craith House to change out of my finery. You know I always wait on tables at Saturday's evening meal.'

'Poor little Cinderella.'

'I really don't mind. Carol and Tom are good to me and it's the least I can do to help out sometimes.'

'I never said it wasn't,' Reece replied gravely. 'So, once that is done and dusted, would you like to come and view a property with me?'

Alexa's face fell.

'You're leaving Craith House?'

He didn't confirm or deny it.

'It's a house for rent that would do for the time I'm here.'

That brought even deeper gloom.

'There's no need to remind me that you're only around for a short time.'

'I wasn't,' he protested mildly. 'Are you coming with me or not?'

'Where is it?'

'In Portinscale, of course.'

That perked her up.

'So you won't be far away.'

'No. Not if I decide to take it, and if I do, I thought I might ask Carol if I could dine at Craith House each evening to save me from malnutrition.'

'Yes, of course I'll go with you,' she said, with the cold front that she'd been hiding behind finally disappearing. 'But in the meantime I must fly, or she'll think I'm not coming. I should be free about half past eight—will that do?'

He nodded, and as she picked her way delicately across the forecourt of the hotel on her high heels, with one hand holding her hat on and the other clutching the handbag that went with her outfit, Alexa had a smile on her face.

Reece was going, but only a short distance away, and if he came in for dinner each evening it wouldn't be very different from how it was now and, she reminded herself, you'll still be seeing him every week day at the practice. What more could you want?

There was an answer to that question, but she wasn't going to pursue it. Not today, anyway.

The house that Reece was considering renting was at the far end of the village. It belonged to a local farmer and had been recently renovated.

As they strolled towards it, both dressed in jeans and sweaters, Alexa discovered that he'd already viewed it once and had more or less decided to take it.

'So why ask for my opinion?' she asked in surprise.

'Well, for one thing, you invariably act and think the opposite way to what I expect. I always get a different slant on things from you.'

'And does that bother you?'

'Er…no…not usually. There is the odd time that you get under my skin, but I can cope.'

'Go on, say it!' she demanded.

'Say what?'

'That in any case you're only passing through, so what does it matter?'

'When I want you to put words into my mouth, Alexa, I'll let you know,' he said flatly, and they walked the rest of the way in silence.

'Well?' Reece asked as they came out of a rambling house built from the familiar Cumberland slate. 'What do you think?'

Alexa looked around her at the tangled garden.

'It's all right, I suppose.'

'Which means that you're not impressed?'

'No. I'm not.'

'Dare I risk commenting that I won't be in it long and that it's clean and weatherproof? Believe me, I've stayed in worse places.'

'Is all this to get away from me?' she asked.

'I beg your pardon! We're together every day at the practice. I'm intending dining at Craith House each night if your sister will allow me...and you think I want to get away from you.

I would probably show more sense if I did. I need a place of my own so that I can entertain if I feel the need.'

'You don't know anyone around here.'

'Of course I do. There's John and Liz...and the staff from the practice.'

'You mean Rebecca?'

'Maybe. But she's not the only one there, is she?'

'No, I suppose not.' She was looking around her and wrinkling her pert nose. 'So you're going to rent it, are you?'

'Yes.'

A footstep behind had them turning, and they found a fair-haired farm hand observing them.

'Hi, there, Lexy,' five feet five of solid muscle said in surprise. 'What brings *you* here? Haven't seen you in ages.'

'I've come to give my opinion on the property. Dr Rowlinson is thinking of renting it,' she said with a friendly smile.

'Yeah, I know. My dad has sent me to see if you've made a decision, sir. As he says, folks are queuing up to view the place.'

'I'm going to take it, I think,' Reece told him, noting that the fellow hadn't taken his gaze off Alexa. It was perhaps as well that it wasn't she who was thinking of living there.

'So how's life been treating you, Lexy?' the man asked of her as they walked to the farm to sort out the rental.

Reece observed him coldly. Lexy! The fellow was making it clear that they weren't strangers. Why didn't he go and plough some furrows or clean out the pigsty?

'Fine,' she told him breezily. 'I finished my training

some time ago and am working at the lakeside practice.'
With a slanting glance at the man by her side she said, 'Dr
Rowlinson works there, too.'

'So you're back in the village for good, then? You should
have let me know. How about us getting together?'

Reece found that he was holding his breath. If she said
yes it would be his fault for bringing Alexa to this
place…and for keeping her at a safe distance. He was a
fool. But he was hardly in a position to suggest that she
tell the blond farmer to get lost.

'Yes, maybe we could some time,' Alexa said easily, as
if she were tuned into Reece's thoughts. 'But I suppose
you're busy harvesting at the moment.'

The fellow laughed. 'Not that busy. I'll give you a ring.'

'That one had some nerve!' Reece said through gritted
teeth as they made their way back to Craith House a little
later.

'Why?' she asked innocently.

'You know why, Alexa,' he told her in the same grim
tone. 'How well do you know him?'

'We were in the same class at school.'

'And because of that he thinks he can start coming on
to you within minutes of meeting?'

'At least Robbie Durkin isn't the sort to run a mile every
time I'm near.'

That brought Reece to a halt in the summer dusk and he
gripped her arm and swung her round to face him. 'Like
me, you mean?'

'If you say so,' she said with a flippancy that was meant
to disguise the effect of his nearness.

'And would you say that I'm running away from you at
this moment?'

'No,' she murmured meekly.

'Right. Then, having clarified that, we'll move on to the
next part of the proceedings, which is being brought about

by jealousy on my part and the fact that your lips are only inches away from mine.'

'Yes, Reece,' she said with the same teasing humility, and would have said more but there wasn't the chance.

He was kissing her as if the world were about to end at any moment, as if the stars above them had come out to applaud, and Alexa knew that it wasn't just a crush that she had on this man, or a capricious desire to make him notice her. It was the real thing. The 'love' thing. And it wasn't going to go away.

Reece let her go at last and as their mouths came apart he sighed. She looked up at him in the quickening dark and there was hurt in her eyes.

'I thought that you were enjoying it as much as I was,' she said quietly. 'Why the sigh? Is it such torture to give in to your feelings? Or maybe it was just jealousy, like you said.'

Craith House and her own little place were showing up blackly against the setting sun and without giving Reece time to answer she fled once more to the sanctuary that they offered.

So much for sense and self-control, Reece told himself as he went up to his room, and all because of that cocky farm-hand. Yet what could he expect? Alexa was young, vibrant, a confident product of her age. It was amazing that she wasn't already attached to some fine young man.

His mouth softened. Yet she seemed to prefer him. The frayed-at-the-ends medic who'd seen more misery than he'd had hot dinners.

Although maybe her affection for him was now in the past if her expression when she'd gone rushing off was anything to go by. He couldn't keep on awakening her senses and then putting her away from him as he had to-night, without putting the blight on her feelings for him.

Tomorrow he would do something about it. He was a fool if he didn't.

He awoke after a restless night to hear the noise of a tractor down below, and when he went to the window his face stretched.

Robbie Durkin was outside, talking to a smiling Alexa, and he reflected that the farmer's son wasn't letting the grass grow under his feet in more ways than one.

Suddenly the excellent breakfast that Carol provided for her guests lost its appeal. As he showered and shaved Reece had to keep reminding himself that he was the one who'd been telling Alexa to find someone of her own age, and now that it looked as if she might be about to do so, he didn't like it.

Yet they both knew that the years between them didn't matter. It was past experiences that made him feel there was such a big difference between them.

It being Sunday, there was no drive into Keswick required. No waiting room full of patients to see. He'd been looking forward to it, but the edge had already gone off the day from the moment he'd seen Alexa's early morning visitor.

By the time he got downstairs the young farmer had gone and Alexa was waiting on tables in the dining room. When she offered him the breakfast menu he looked up, and as their eyes met food became a thing of no importance, compared to what was in his mind.

'I see you've had a visitor,' he said flatly.

She smiled. Just the mere sight of the man looking up at her had brought a glow to the day, and the previous night's disappointing ending seemed less hurtful in the light of morning.

'Yes. But I didn't let Robbie stay long. He'd been muck-spreading in the top pasture and he smelt rather ripe.'

'I see.'

'So when are you moving out?' she asked.

'Some time today, I suppose, while I've got the time. Though it's only a matter of packing my cases.'

'Does Carol know you're going?'

'Yes, and she's agreed that I can dine here each evening, so I'll still be around to annoy you.'

'You don't annoy me, Reece,' she said with her accustomed candour. 'You frustrate me.'

'Because I don't let you have things all your own way?'

'No. Because all the time you think you know best.'

She brushed an imaginary crumb off the table.

'I hope that you get settled into your new accommodation all right. I won't be around to assist as I'm going on the lake with Robbie this afternoon and then we're going for a meal.'

'So you're not on duty here, then?'

Alexa shook her head.

'No. Not tonight.' And on that negative note she disappeared into the kitchen.

Robbie Durkin had been at agricultural college for the last three years and Alexa hadn't known he was back in Portinscale until the previous evening.

They'd been in the same class at school and had been on reasonably good terms, although he'd always been rather big-headed. Now, after last night's meeting, it seemed as if the young farmer wanted to become better acquainted.

She hoped he wasn't going to get any wrong ideas, but it was a nice feeling to have someone eager for her company.

Not that Reece didn't seek her out sometimes, but she always felt that he did it against his better judgement, and nothing could be more dampening than that.

When she thought how suddenly her life had changed it was incredible. At the beginning of the summer she'd been happy in a carefree sort of way. Content with her job at the practice, and in her spare time having the odd date with guys who were pleasant enough to be with but didn't make her heart beat faster.

And now what? On a sunny afternoon she'd swum out into the lake to rescue a couple of foolish kids. While she'd been so engaged a stranger had come to their aid and her life had changed for ever.

After breakfast Reece walked to the marina at the end of the village and picked up the first passenger boat across the lake to Keswick.

He had decided that if Alexa intended spending the day with the fellow they'd met last night, he might as well put his time to some use by going into the surgery for a few hours. There would still be plenty of time to move his belongings into his new accommodation when he got back.

There were parts of the practice that he still had to familiarise himself with and paperwork to bring up to date that Bryan had passed on to him, so it wouldn't be a wasted journey.

As he let himself into the quiet rooms, which tomorrow would be bustling with staff and patients, he gazed around him thoughtfully.

If he'd decided to spend the next few months somewhere else, instead of letting John persuade him to come to this place, his mind wouldn't be in such turmoil, he told himself.

But then he wouldn't have got to know Alexa and that was something he couldn't bear to have missed. Even if she didn't do anything for his peace of mind and strength of purpose.

A mental picture presented itself of her sitting in the rowing boat from Craith House with the muscle-bound Durkin guy seated opposite as he plied the oars.

What would they do when they got to the other side? he wondered. Stroll around the shops before they went to eat, and then walk beside the lake beneath the setting sun?

'Forget her!' he told himself out loud. 'You've come here to work, not daydream.' And with that thought in mind he positioned himself behind his desk.

'Did you see Reece go out?' Alexa asked of Carol when they'd cleared away after breakfast.

Her sister nodded.

'Yes. He went towards the marina.'

'How strange. He's moving into the house belonging to the Durkins today. I would have expected him to be going in that direction.'

'Well, he wasn't,' Carol assured her. 'I presumed he was going to catch the boat to Keswick.'

'Why?'

'I really don't know, Alexa. When he comes back you can ask him.'

'Mmm, I suppose so,' she murmured absently.

She'd spent the last hour wishing that she hadn't arranged to go out with Robbie. If she spent the day with anyone she wanted it to be Reece, but for some reason he'd made a quick getaway before she'd had a chance to change her plans.

But Keswick wasn't so large a place. If she followed the regular tourist routes she might find him, and no sooner had come the thought than she was planning the deed.

'Robbie isn't picking me up until three o'clock,' she told Carol, 'which gives me five hours.'

'For what?'

'To find Reece.'

'And then what?'

'I don't know, but I won't let Robbie down. It wouldn't be fair.'

Carol sighed. 'Oh, what a tangled web you're weaving.'

'I'm not!' Alexa protested. 'I'm just giving out signals.'

'Who to, though?'

'Reece of course.' Her mouth drooped. 'I'm in love with him, Caro.'

'Yes, I know you are, little sister,' she said gently, 'but you could get hurt. That man has been around. He's seen and done things that you would only encounter in your worst nightmares.'

CHAPTER FIVE

As Alexa waited for the next sailing across the lake, she knew that she could have driven or walked into Keswick, but this was the route she loved the most and if it was the direction that Reece had taken she was more likely to find him somewhere along the way.

Yet common sense told her that she was on a fool's errand, rushing off after him when she hadn't a clue what he had in mind or where he was going.

He wouldn't have gone to see John as he and Liz had gone away for a couple of weeks. But there was nothing to say that he hadn't gone walking, or used local transport to take him into Ambleside where he'd been brought up.

It was typical of her supreme optimism that she should expect to find him amongst the seasonal crowds thronging the area.

But, of course, it didn't work out like that. There wasn't a sign of him anywhere. Until, wandering disconsolately past the surgery, she saw a shadow against one of the windows.

Her step faltered. They'd had a couple of attempted break-ins recently, crazy hopefuls expecting to find a cabinet full of drugs inside, and there was nothing to say that another one wasn't in progress.

But not if she could help it!

The door swung open as she pushed it gently inwards and she stepped into the passage with heartbeats quickening. She could hear voices in the room at the end that had been allocated to Reece, and before she lost her nerve and fled, Alexa marched in.

As the man and woman inside observed her in startled amazement Alexa knew beyond doubt that she was on a fool's errand.

Reece had his arm around Rebecca's shoulders and she was leaning against him, seductive and suppliant. If she'd been giving off steam instead of her usual cold iciness Alexa wouldn't have been surprised.

'Oops! Sorry!' she said with an attempt at flippancy. 'I didn't know the surgery was open on Sundays. Somebody should have told me.' She watched Reece slowly remove his arm from around the blonde doctor. 'Or maybe not.'

'What has brought you here, Alexa?' he said levelly as he seated himself behind the desk.

'In the first instance the boat, secondly my feet, and thirdly the thought that a break-in might be taking place,' she informed him blandly.

His face stretched. 'And you were going to subdue the burglars all by yourself, were you?'

She felt sick with dismay, but there was no way Reece was going to know that. 'Not if there were more than two,' she retaliated, still trying for the flippant approach.

Rebecca was straightening her hair and picking up her bag, and with the frost returning she said, 'I'll see you both tomorrow.'

Alexa took a step back. 'Don't go because of me, Dr. Soames. I've come in to Keswick to do some shopping, so I'll be off.'

Reece was raising his hand as if to detain her, but she wasn't having any and with a swing of slender hips and a toss of long chestnut locks she went.

As she waited for the boat to take her back to Portinscale, Alexa was overwhelmed with mortification. She'd gone chasing after Reece without pride or dignity and had been well and truly put in her place.

And what a strange episode it had been. Two of the

partners meeting in secret at the practice. Why couldn't they be open about what was going on between them? Neither of them were committed to anyone else as far as she knew. Obviously Reece was practising what he preached and had gone for the more mature charms of Rebecca Soames.

Her face burned at the memory of the night before on their way back from the Durkins' farm. He hadn't been backward at coming forward then, had he? It would appear that she was the programme for light entertainment, while Rebecca was…what?

She could see the boat coming back from the other side of the lake, and as she walked along the wooden jetty with the rest of those who were waiting, a voice said from behind, 'Save me a seat, Alexa.'

Without turning, she said sweetly, 'Find your own.'

It was a vain gesture as the boat was going to be half-empty, and no sooner had she settled onto one of the long wooden seats than Reece was beside her.

'So what was all that about?' he asked as the craft began to cut through the water.

'What? Me catching you with Rebecca in the surgery?'

'Catching me!' he hooted. 'You make it sound very furtive.'

'So? If the cap fits…'

'The cap doesn't fit, Alexa. The only catching involved was me catching up with my paperwork. I had foreseen a long empty day ahead of me, and who should appear but Rebecca?'

'So what was it that I walked in on, then? A consultation?'

He was smiling. 'You really are the limit.'

'I'm not asking for a diagnosis,' she snapped. 'And don't change the subject.'

'Rebecca was upset because she's in a rented house

where the lease will soon be up and she has nowhere to go. I was merely offering comfort.'

'And did she volunteer that information just after you'd told her that you were about to move to a huge rambling place that was going to be far too big for just one person?'

'Yes. As a matter of fact she did,' he said in assumed surprise. 'How did you guess?'

Alexa got to her feet. 'If you're going to start poking fun, I'm going to—'

'What? Jump overboard?'

'No. Change my seat.'

He took her arm and eased her back down beside him.

'So far you've been asking all the questions,' he said with the smile still playing around his mouth. 'Now it's my turn. What were you doing in Keswick? Had you really gone to shop? Or was there another reason?'

She couldn't be bothered to lie.

'I'd gone looking for you.'

'Why?'

It was still a moment for truth.

'I was missing you.'

He was laughing now.

'But you'd seen me at breakfast time.'

'What? With you glued to the menu and me skipping around the tables in my waitress outfit? But you're not going to sidetrack me. Are you attracted to Rebecca Soames?'

'Does it matter?'

Alexa sighed. 'Don't fence with me, Reece. You know it does.'

'I thought that you were on the brink of a new relationship yourself with the young farmer,' he fired back. 'He was round sharp enough this morning on that huge tractor thing, and you've made arrangements to see him later.'

Her colour was rising and it deepened even more when he went on to say, 'But far be it from me to pass judgement.

I've kept telling you to find someone more suitable…more your own kind.'

'That's just it!' she flared. 'You *are* passing judgement, by assuming that you know who my own kind are. I would think that I'm the best judge of that.'

The landing stage was looming up and he was saved from having to answer, but as she walked ahead of him up the wooden gangplank he called, 'Slow down, Alexa. Every time we come to this place you end up rushing off for some reason or another. Is it too much to ask that we walk back to Craith House side by side?'

Alexa didn't know whether to laugh or cry. The day was going from bad to worse. She hadn't missed the fact that Reece still hadn't answered her question about Rebecca.

Obviously there was no reason why he should if he didn't want to, but she knew he was hedging by the way he'd switched the conversation to Robbie Durkin and herself.

Perversely she slowed her stride in answer to his request, and for the rest of the way they moved at a snail's pace, with Alexa stony-faced and the man beside her lapsing into silence.

When they got to Craith House it was the inevitable parting of the ways again, with Alexa going to her own apartment and Reece making his way upstairs to start packing. Should he ask Rebecca to share the house with him? he wondered as he gathered his belongings together. He didn't want to. For one thing she wasn't his type, and for another, far more important, it wouldn't do much for his relationship with Alexa, who would read more into it than was intended.

Yet if the woman was soon going to be homeless it seemed like the least he could do. He was wishing now that he hadn't decided to move. It would have been simpler to have stayed here at Craith House where a certain young nurse was based.

Simpler, yes, but not wise, he told himself. Wasn't he supposed to be behaving sensibly where Alexa was concerned during the coming months?

In the process of folding one of his shirts he became still as the memory of how she'd felt in his arms the night before came back. With a frustrated sigh he threw it down onto the bed and went to stand by the window.

His timing wasn't good. In a repetition of the morning Robbie Durkin was down there again with a smug smile on his face, and as Reece looked down on him Alexa appeared in a low-cut green dress that made her hair look like dark copper and her skin as smooth as alabaster.

He caught his breath. She was beautiful and carefree. What had *he* to offer her with his jaundiced views on love and marriage?

She and Durkin made a handsome pair. So why couldn't he be happy for them? The answer wasn't hard to seek. He wanted her for himself.

Picking up the discarded shirt, he flung it into his suitcase and with lips compressed he zipped it up and fastened the straps. He was doing the right thing in moving out, he told himself, and tomorrow he would ask Rebecca if she wanted to share the house at the Durkins' farm with him.

Keswick had been busy in the morning, but by the middle of the afternoon, with a warm summer sun high in the sky, both the lake and the paths around it were full of tourists and local folk.

'So what's with you and the doctor fellow that you were with last night?' Robbie asked as they looked around for seats in a wine bar later in the evening.

'Nothing,' Alexa told him, trying to keep the regret out of her voice. 'Reece has agreed to work as locum at the practice for six months as a favour to John, and he's been staying at Craith House.'

'Seems strange for a guy like that to be working as a temp,' he said dubiously.

'That's because he's taking a break from working abroad in under-developed countries,' she said quickly, resenting the implied critisism.

'Oh. I see,' he murmured vaguely. Catching sight of a group of his friends, he steered her towards them with his arm possessively around her waist.

'Who's this, Robbie?' a lanky young fellow with a shaved head and gold earrings asked, leering at Alexa.

She eyed him glacially. 'I'm quite capable of answering for myself. My name's Alexa Howard.'

'We were in the same class at school and have just met up again,' Robbie told him, tightening his grip on her. His eyes went over the rest of the group. 'So what have we got planned for tonight?'

'A pub crawl and then a party at my place,' a blonde girl said in an incredibly loud voice.

This is a big mistake, Alexa was thinking. She'd out-grown this sort of thing. They might all be of a similar age chronologically, but she felt years older than this noisy bunch that Robbie seemed to hang out with.

However, she'd agreed to spend the evening with him and would have to put up with it. For one thing, she'd no transport back. The last ferry across the lake would be go-ing any second and likewise the last bus, but she supposed there was always a taxi if she became desperate.

It was a quarter to midnight and she'd had enough. Robbie and his friends had all been drinking steadily and were now pointing themselves in the direction of the blonde girl's flat.

'I'd rather go straight home if you don't mind,' Alexa told him. 'I have to be up early in the morning and this isn't really my scene.'

'No way!' he protested. 'It's too early. You'll like it when we get there, Lexy. You'll see.'

'I want to go home, Robbie,' she insisted, and now he was getting rattled.

'All right, but don't expect me to go with you,' he growled.

'I don't,' she told him calmly, and before he could protest any further she'd gone, walking quickly in the direction of the taxi rank.

It was a wasted exercise. There wasn't a cab in sight and, after waiting a quarter of an hour, Alexa decided that she would walk the short distance to Portinscale.

When she got to the outskirts of Keswick where the road veered off towards the fields, she strode briskly through the warm night along paths that she'd trodden for as long as she could remember.

There was no moon, only a starlit sky above, but she wasn't nervous. This land was as familiar as the nose on her face, and soon she was crossing the narrow suspension bridge only yards away from Craith House.

Her feet echoed hollowly on its wooden planking and after a few seconds she realised that she wasn't the only one on the bridge. Someone was behind her, walking with a heavier footstep than her own, and for a moment she was uneasy.

But the end of the structure was in sight and as she stepped off it streetlamps and the floodlit grounds of a nearby hotel were banishing the dark.

The footsteps behind were increasing their pace, and as she turned to see who it was a voice that she recognised immediately exclaimed, 'Alexa! What on earth are you doing out here on your own? Where's Durkin?'

'We were invited to a party, but I didn't want to go,' she said awkwardly as Reece came into view.

'And he left you to come home alone at this hour?' he questioned grimly.

'Er…yes, but I don't mind. I went for a taxi but there weren't any.'

'Well, I *do* mind, and I shall tell him so the next time I see him.'

'What are you doing here?' she retaliated. 'I would have thought you'd be tucked up in your new house by now.'

'I *am* in residence,' he informed her with the anger still in him, 'but I take it that I'm still allowed a late night stroll by the lake?'

Alexa could see the lights of Craith House only yards away and this time she was in no hurry to go inside, not when Reece was standing so close.

For some reason she felt tearful. Not because he was angry at finding her walking home alone late at night. That was oddly comforting. But because he'd been in her thoughts all the time she'd been with Robbie and his friends and now he was actually here, observing her with a mixture of concern and irritation.

'Yes, of course you are,' she said softly. As they began to walk side by side she added, 'You love the lakes, don't you, Reece?'

He nodded, his face sombre.

'You've no idea how many times I've clung on to thoughts of Cumbria when I've been surrounded with sickness and squalor.'

'What made you decide to work abroad?' Alexa asked in the same gentle tone.

He gave a wry smile.

'A desire to put my training to the very best possible use …which resulted in a broken engagement.'

'You were engaged?'

Envy was washing over her. Who was the woman he'd been engaged to?

She was about to find out.

'Do you want to hear about it?'

'Of course. If you feel like talking about it.'

'I don't, but you might hear it from someone else if I don't tell you. Although I don't expect you to find it of much interest.'

'Try me,' she said quietly, and braced herself for what was to come.

'Natalie Bracknell's parents are wealthy farmers,' he said sombrely. 'They had a spread near Lake Buttermere and more or less led the social scene in the area, which suited their beautiful only daughter down to the ground.'

So she was beautiful, Alexa thought ruefully...and rich. Not a nondescript nurse at the local surgery.

Observing her downcast expression, Reece's face softened. Natalie wasn't as beautiful as the bronze-haired temptress beside him, he thought achingly.

'So what happened?' she was asking, trying not to sound too curious.

'Our parents were friends, which threw Natalie and me together a lot and we fell in love. Or at least I did. Looking back, I wonder just exactly why she went along with it.

'She was pleasure-loving, demanding and sometimes completely irresponsible in the way she behaved. We were as different as chalk from cheese, but I was attracted to her and hoped she would change once we were married.'

He paused and, desperate to hear the rest, Alexa prompted, 'And?'

Reece laughed and it grated harshly.

'I've questioned since if hers was arrested personality development, or if the fault was mine because I was too absorbed in my career.

'Anyway, shortly after we'd become engaged I had the chance to work abroad for a couple of years in one of the under-developed countries. I was very keen to do so and hoped that Natalie would understand how much it meant to me.

'She didn't. Spoilt and used to getting her own way, she made a huge fuss. Her argument was that if I loved her she should come first and, caring for her as I did, it seemed only right that I should give way.

'But on the point of refusing the offer I made a sickening discovery. Whether out of pique, petulance or just plain promiscuity, she was having an affair with a wealthy business friend of her father's. He was older than both of us and had been around…which, I suppose, made him more her type than a dedicated young doctor who had dared to have other things on his mind besides an unpredictable fiancée. After that I had no doubts as to where my future lay and it wasn't in these parts. I don't know how she felt about me going, but as far as I was concerned she had made her bed and could lie on it.

'As for me, I knew I hadn't come out of the break-up unscathed. I'd lost my appetite for falling in love.'

'And where is she now?' Alexa questioned, feeling as if she were fighting her way through a thick grey mist.

'She married the fellow, but I'm told they've divorced and that she's living back with her parents.'

'Which is where?' she croaked as the thought of an attractive ex-fiancée in the neighbourhood took her spirits down to zero.

'They're still living in the same place, near Lake Buttermere,' he informed her carefully. 'Does it matter?'

'Er…no…of course not,' she fibbed. 'But who told you where she was? You must have asked.'

'John told me and, yes, I did ask.'

'Why?'

He was smiling in the darkness.

'That's for me to know and you to find out.'

As she turned away disconsolately, for once lost for

words, he put his arms around her. With her head nestling beneath his chin, he said softly, 'Don't start imagining things that aren't there, Alexa. Everyone has a past.'

He bent and brushed her smooth brow with his lips.

'I'm going to see you to the door, which is more than Durkin did. Then I'm off to spend my first night on that young upstart's doorstep, and I shall be taking note of what time he arrives home and who with... And if you think I sound like an over-protective father, don't believe it. I care about...my friends.'

He was releasing her, and with her fire gone out she didn't protest.

'Goodnight, Reece,' she said limply, resisting the urge to tell him that she didn't give a damn who Robbie came home with.

More important was that Reece had come back to the lakes where his ex-fiancée was now living and had obviously been keen to know her whereabouts. Was Natalie the reason why he'd agreed to do six months at the lakeside practice?

He hadn't forgotten this girl. She'd seen how his face had softened when he'd said that she was beautiful.

Why on earth had he gone bleating on about Natalie Bracknell? Reece was asking himself irritably as he walked to the end of the village and his new abode.

He'd been right in thinking that Alexa would want to know about her, but he needn't have obliged. What was she thinking now? he wondered. That he was here to stir up the old porridge?

Talking about Natalie had brought back past hurts again, although for a long time she had been just a shadowy figure amongst the painful memories.

Before he had started at the practice, John had mentioned that her father had been in to see him. Reece had asked after the daughter, but it certainly hadn't been with any longing to renew the acquaintance.

As he put the key in the lock of the old farm cottage he told himself that it would have been simpler not to have come back to the lakes.

Yet the sight of Alexa stepping off the suspension bridge onto the main street of the village had brought a brighter end to a dismal day, though it hadn't stopped him from feeling angry that she'd been left to walk home alone at such a late hour.

No doubt she'd done it before and would do it again, but the sight of the slender girl in the green dress, alone in the dark night, had brought forth such a surge of protective tenderness inside him that he'd found his heart hammering and his loins aching from the force of it.

The house smelt musty when he went inside and he cursed himself for a fool. Why hadn't he stayed in the warmth and cleanliness of Craith House?

He was running away from Alexa, that was why. They had to work with each other at the surgery, but at least here he would be away from the chemistry that had been there between them from the moment of meeting.

The week that followed the distracting Sunday was no different than any other, with full waiting rooms at the surgery, queues to see the nurses and the usual number of house calls.

Alexa noted that Reece and Rebecca seemed to be on the best of terms after he'd listened to her tale of woe in the deserted practice on Sunday morning, and if she'd had any doubts about it, what Beryl had to tell her one morning would have banished them immediately.

She was testing the blood pressure of a patient who'd come in for a regular check-up and was on the point of telling her that it was dangerously high when Beryl came in and said, 'A word when you're free, Alexa.'

Alexa nodded and, turning back to the woman who was eyeing her anxiously, she said, 'I'm afraid that you're going to have to see one of the doctors, Mrs Reade. It's quite high. Have you been feeling unwell at all?'

'I've had some funny headaches lately,' the middle-aged librarian admitted, 'but apart from that I've felt all right.'

'Yes. I see. Well, we'll see what the doctor has to say. The reading I'm getting is way above normal. If you go to Reception they'll tell you which doctor is free to see you.'

As the woman went to do her bidding Alexa's expression was solemn. Mary Reade would be lucky if she didn't find herself sent straight to hospital when she saw one of the partners.

Before Beryl could buttonhole her, Reece came striding into the nurse's room and said, 'I've sent for an ambulance for Mrs Reade and phoned her daughter who lives just down the road to pack a bag and meet her here. With blood pressure as high as that, she could have a stroke at any time.'

'Are you all right, Alexa?' he asked, noting that she was lacking lustre. 'I haven't seen anything of you the last few nights when I've gone to Craith House for my evening meal.'

'I'm fine,' she said breezily, not wanting him to know that she'd been in the doldrums ever since hearing about his ex-fiancée being in the neighbourhood.

She was discovering that loving him was a wearing business. Defeatism wasn't normally part of her personality, but she was beginning to realise that every time she thought her relationship with Reece was moving onto a firmer footing, it slid back.

Maybe it was because his ex-fiancée wasn't far away. Or

because he was so friendly with Rebecca, when all Reece had for herself were admonitions to get on with her life.

Yet he wasn't averse to taking an interest in that same life. She'd heard from Robbie Durkin that Reece had collared him on Monday morning and given him a rollicking for letting her walk home alone.

'Fancies you himself, does he?' the farmer's son had said snappily. 'Didn't you tell your doctor friend that it was your choice to come home early?'

'Yes, I did,' she'd told him defensively. 'But Reece *did* have a point. You *did* leave me high and dry in Keswick...and I couldn't find a taxi.'

His colour had risen. 'I'm...er...I'm sorry, Lexy. How about giving me another chance?'

She'd smiled to take the sting out of her refusal. 'No thanks, Robbie. We don't move in the same circles any more.'

It was true, they didn't. She'd found Robbie and his friends noisy and childish. But that being so, what circles did she move in? Not the same ones as a doctor who was in her every waking thought.

Her face softened. Reece cared enough to be concerned about her safety. That was something. It was what friendship was about. Maybe she ought to settle for that.

It was lunchtime before Alexa got a chance to talk to the older practice nurse, and what Beryl had to say did nothing to raise her spirits.

'I heard Rebecca telling Bryan that she's moving in with Reece Rowlinson next week when her lease is up. What do you think of that?'

'Not a lot,' Alexa said flatly, 'but I'm not surprised. She was dropping hints when I saw them together on Sunday. Reece has moved into that rented house at the Durkins' farm and there's lots of space, so I suppose it follows that he would offer.'

He didn't have to, though, did he, she thought as she drove home that night. But he was entitled to please himself and, no doubt, would continue to do so.

Reece had commented that she hadn't been around at Craith House in the evenings. Well, tonight she would be, if only to see if he told her about his new house partner.

Her presence was opportune. Carol had a migraine and Alexa told her, 'Go to bed, Caro. I'll wait on tables if Tom will dish up.'

When she appeared at his side in the dining room Reece smiled.

'Ah! So tonight you're not conspicuous by your absence.'

Suddenly light-hearted, she beamed down onto his dark crop.

'I'm sure that you haven't missed me. After all, we're in each other's orbit all day. I would expect you to have seen enough of me by this time of night.'

He laughed low in his throat.

'It's a different thing when we're away from the surgery, Alexa. We both know that. Come and walk with me at our favourite place by the lake when you've finished. Say eight o'clock down by the marina?'

'Yes, all right,' she said softly, unable to refuse such a request.

But it didn't stop her from wondering if they would be magical moments in the summer dusk or a discussion about Rebecca's pending removal.

After the guests had been served, Alexa and her amiable brother-in-law sat down at the kitchen table to eat their own meal. All the time they were eating she had her eye on the clock.

'I'll clear away,' Tom said when they'd finished. 'You've been on your feet all day, Alexa.'

'I've got time to stack the dishwasher,' she told him, 'but I'll go after that, if you don't mind.'

To be alone with Reece was like paradise beckoning. It seemed an eternity since he'd followed her across the suspension bridge on Sunday night and expressed his annoyance at her solitary state.

She ached for the clean maleness of him. His touch, his mouth on hers, being cradled close to the comforting strength of him. Would he ever want her to that extent?

There'd been no emotion in his voice when Reece had told her about his broken engagement, but even in the short time they'd known each other she'd become accustomed to his moods and motivations and Alexa knew that he'd been hurt badly by it.

As a young, enthusiastic idealist, he'd been ready to change his plans for Natalie Bracknell, but he'd found her to be faithless and undeserving.

Reece was idly skimming flat pebbles across the lake's surface when she found him. He turned quickly at the sound of her footsteps on the shale and his heart skipped a beat.

Alexa Howard was the loveliest thing he'd ever seen, standing before him in a tangerine halter-neck cotton top and the briefest of white shorts.

Her legs were long and shapely, her breasts full and rounded in the skimpy top, and it was there again, the longing that she aroused in him.

Yet only seconds before he'd been berating himself for asking her to meet him, knowing he'd made the request out of pure selfishness because he wanted her to himself for a little while. Away from the public who everlastingly demanded their attention at the surgery, and away from her nice relations.

He needed Alexa's bright spirit. The uncomplicated, outgoing charm that was just as much her as the hard-working, dedicated nurse.

He took a step towards her, desire rising in him like a warm tide, but in that second Reece realised that they weren't alone. A silver sports car had pulled up only yards away and a voice that he hadn't heard in a long time was calling, 'Reece! They said I would find you here.'

At the sound of a strange voice Alexa turned slowly. The main road through the village was only yards away from the lakeside where they'd arranged to meet, and a car had pulled off it into their special place.

The woman who was getting out of it was small and golden blonde, with an attractive face that was spoilt by a petulant mouth.

Alexa couldn't see the labels on her clothes but it was clear that they weren't off the peg. The car, the clothes and the jewellery that was glittering in the last of the sun's rays were all signs of wealth, but none of that mattered.

It was the familiarity in her manner as she called across to Reece that was making Alexa's insides knot, and they tightened even more as he began to walk slowly towards the newcomer.

'Natalie!' he said quietly. 'How are you? It's been a long time.'

'Too long,' she cooed. 'It was only today that Daddy said he'd been talking to John Hendrix and the old guy had told him you were coming back. Otherwise I'd have looked you up sooner.'

I'll bet! Alexa thought grimly.

Even if Reece hadn't said the woman's name she would have known who she was. Everything about her fitted the bill...including her cheek!

He was turning towards herself with an expression that was giving nothing away.

'Allow me to introduce Alexa Howard, Natalie. Alexa is

a friend of mine and also a colleague at the practice. I've been staying at her sister's guest house until recently.'

His ex-fiancée threw a brief nod in Alexa's direction and then with eyes narrowing, asked, 'And where are you based now?'

'I'm renting a house belonging to Durkins' Farm.'

'You could have stayed with us.' She pouted.

'Your place is too far away, I'm afraid,' he told her in a voice that was as lacking in expression as his face. 'I need to be near the surgery.'

She shrugged narrow shoulders.

'So when are we going to get together to talk about old times? Now?'

Alexa found herself holding her breath. The blonde predator wasn't wasting any time! Surely Reece wasn't going to let this manipulative, hard-boiled woman into his life again!

'Why not?' he agreed blandly. 'If Alexa will excuse us.'

'Yes, of course,' she said coolly, trying not to choke on her disbelief.

He was opening the door on the passenger side of the car and slotting himself in beside the woman he'd once hoped to marry. As the vehicle began to move away he said, 'I'll see you later, Alexa.'

Not if I can help it, she vowed as she turned towards home.

CHAPTER SIX

'REECE called late last night,' Carol said the next morning.

'He didn't knock on *my* door,' Alexa said flatly.

'No, he didn't,' her sister agreed. 'He came to see if you were here as all your lights were out, which, I suppose, wasn't surprising as it was well past midnight.'

'That man has some nerve!' she cried. 'Did he think I would be sitting there, waiting for him to spare me a moment of his precious time, after he'd gone waltzing off with an old girlfriend?'

'Do I take it that he's not your favourite man today?' Carol asked with a sympathetic glance at Alexa's set face.

'No, he's not,' she admitted as she picked up her car keys. 'He's too busy keeping his fan club in order.'

'Er…fan club?' Carol questioned.

'Yes. Rebecca Soames and an ex-fiancée who has reared her golden head.'

'Really?'

'Yes, Carol, really!' And with that she marched off to see what awaited her at the practice.

Reece was there before her, chatting amicably with the other two doctors before surgery commenced, but when she appeared he followed her into the nurse's room.

'I called at your place last night,' he said, 'but you must have been asleep.'

'So I believe,' she said tonelessly. 'Carol told me. Were you expecting me to wait up?'

'Not exactly. I just hoped that you might have done, as I had something to tell you.'

'Such as you've found yourself a house mate?'

'No, not that, though it is a fact. In view of Rebecca's problem I said she could move into my place for a few weeks if she wanted.'

'And did she want?'

'Er...yes...for the time being.'

'I see.'

'Why the long face?'

'Last night you asked me to meet you down by the lake. It was your suggestion...not mine. But the moment your ex-fiancée turned up, you were off like a rocket. How do you think I felt? Certainly not in the mood for waiting until you could find time for me.'

He patted her cheek gently.

'I know. But I had my reasons, Alexa. I didn't want her to—'

He didn't finish the sentence. Beryl had come bustling in with her mind on other things and she didn't notice the sudden silence.

'I'll speak to you later, Alexa,' Reece said briefly, and off he went.

'I'm down for helping Dr Rowlinson with the asthma clinic this afternoon,' the older woman said when he'd gone. 'I would have thought that you'd have been more his choice.'

'Apparently not,' Alexa said levelly, and went to tell the next person in the queue outside that she was ready for them.

Jackie Bellingham had chronic asthma and had been on steroids for many years, with the result that her skin was paper-thin. The slightest knock broke the surface, and today she had come to have a fresh dressing on an ulcerated leg which had been caused by just a minor scratch.

It wasn't the first time that Jackie had suffered this sort

of thing and it wouldn't be the last. She was caught in a vicious circle.

Without the steroids she would be gasping for breath, and with them there was the serious problem of the deteriorating condition of her skin.

But she was only one of many patients who had to put up with unpleasant side-effects to get relief from something else.

To Alexa's surprise she was followed by Kirsten Clark, the young girl who'd had the heart attack in the nurse's room on Reece's first day at the practice.

'What can I do for you, Kirsten?' she asked with the special smile that she reserved for nervous patients.

The girl swallowed.

'I've come to thank you for what you did for me when I was taken ill. My mum says I would have died if it hadn't been for you and the new doctor.'

Alexa's smile flashed out again. 'You certainly gave us a fright.'

'He went with us all the way in the ambulance and I'd like to thank him, too.'

'I'm sure that Dr Rowlinson will be pleased to see you. Hang on and I'll see if I can find him.'

'Someone to see you,' she said briefly as Reece waited for his next patient to appear.

'Not Natalie?'

Alexa shook her head in gloomy wonder. The woman hadn't been back in his life five minutes and she was the first person that came to his mind.

'No. It's Kirsten Clark,' she said flatly. 'The girl who had the cardiac arrest on your first day here. She wants to thank you.'

He was on his feet.

'Lead on. I've just time for a quick word before my next sufferer appears.'

As she watched him with the blushing schoolgirl, Alexa thought that if ever a man was in the right profession Reece was. Kirsten was telling him that she might have to have an operation and he was giving her his full attention, as if she were the only patient who mattered…and as far as he was concerned, at that moment she was.

By the time he'd finished talking to her, Reece's next patient was waiting, and as the day took its course their paths didn't cross again.

Alexa told herself that he could have found time for a brief word if he really had something to tell her, but as he wasn't making the effort it couldn't be that important.

She thought he might turn up some time during the evening but he didn't present himself, and when she saw his car go past in the direction of Buttermere her spirits took a further downward plunge.

There was only one reason why he would be going in that direction. Natalie Bracknell, who, it would appear, was anxious to rekindle old fires, and if he wanted to warm himself there he could get on with it.

The main topic amongst the staff at the practice was the sponsored walk for charity which they'd all pledged themselves to do on the coming Saturday.

It was scheduled to start at half past ten as one of the nurses and a doctor had to be on duty for the brief emergency surgery that was held every Saturday morning.

In this instance it was Alexa and Reece, an arrangement that would normally have pleased her, but now it loomed ahead as another occasion that almost certainly wouldn't take them in the direction that she wanted to go.

Everyone was taking part in the walk and when Reece had first heard about it he'd said enthusiastically, 'The route is over my happy hunting ground of long ago. I can't wait to walk through the Newlands Valley and climb Catbells.'

The weather on Saturday morning wasn't good. The mountains were hidden in mist, the sky above the village leaden and there was a fine drizzle.

When she drew back her curtains Alexa pulled a wry face. There had been day after day of warm, dry weather, but not today. But the arrangements had been made. The walk would take place. The staff of the lakeside practice were committed to it.

As she packed a rucksack with her walking gear and provisions, her spirits were bouncing back. Whatever else, she was determined to enjoy the day, even though it was going to be with a dozen or so other folk and the likelihood of spending some prime time with Reece was remote.

But first there was morning surgery to deal with, and maybe by the time it was over the weather would have improved.

The receptionist on duty gave a rueful smile when Alexa appeared.

'Ghastly morning for the hike,' she remarked.

'Isn't it just?' Alexa agreed. With a look around the empty waiting room she said, 'Is this how it's going to be, I wonder? Or are the Saturday morning patients a bit slow in getting mobile today?'

'It's early yet,' the other woman said. 'Give them time. Dr Rowlinson isn't here yet.'

'He is,' Reece said from the doorway, and as he stepped to one side a mother appeared with a small boy who looked hot and feverish, and behind them was a man with his hand wrapped in a towel.

'It would appear that we're in business,' he said with a smile. 'Shall we get the show under way, Alexa?'

She wanted to smile back. In khaki shorts and a dark blue sweatshirt he looked a far cry from the GP the patients would be expecting to see. In contrast, she was in her uniform, intending to change the moment surgery was over.

'Mr Jameson has scalded his hand, Alexa,' Reece said when he came into her room minutes later, closely followed by the man she'd seen earlier. 'He has mistakenly put butter on it and it's badly blistered. It needs cleaning first and then a non-stick dressing.'

Alexa nodded and, indicating for the patient to sit down, took the man's big paw in hers. Reece was hovering. Looking up at him, she said, 'When do you want Mr Jameson back to have it looked at, Dr Rowlinson?'

'Monday,' he said briefly, and she sensed that his attention was being diverted.

In the next second she knew why. A high-pitched voice, which was vaguely familiar, was demanding outside in the corridor, 'I want to see Dr Rowlinson. Immediately!'

'Excuse me,' he said quickly, and before she could reply he was departing in the direction of the strident tones.

By the time Alexa had dealt with the scalded hand all was quiet again, and when she went into Reception the girl there said, 'Did you hear all the noise a few moments ago? It was someone demanding to see Dr Rowlinson. She *was* in a state!'

At that moment the door of his consulting room opened and Alexa became still. She might have known. It was the autocratic Natalie who had been making all the fuss. Who did she think she was? Barging into the surgery without an appointment.

'You remember Natalie,' he said smoothly as his blonde companion dabbed at her eyes with a flimsy handkerchief.

'Yes, of course,' Alexa told him stiffly. She wasn't likely to forget how this woman had demanded his attention within minutes of meeting and totally ignored her. And now she'd monopolised him again. 'Determined' was the word that sprang to mind.

Reece was steering his ex-fiancée towards the door and

Alexa went back to her room where there were still people waiting to be seen.

One of them was Mary Reade, who only the day before had been discharged from hospital with her blood pressure now under control.

'I'm a walking disaster at the moment, Nurse,' she said ruefully. 'This morning my garden path was slippery with the rain and I fell and twisted my ankle. I was dreading having broken it, but Dr Rowlinson doesn't think so. He's sent me to you to have it bandaged.'

Alexa was checking the patient's notes. 'Yes, he says that it's just a sprain and a cold compress and bandaging is all that's required.'

By the time she'd seen the last patient on their way the staff had arrived, suitably clothed for the occasion, most of them good-humoured in spite of the weather.

Though it didn't seem to be washing off onto Rebecca. She was huddled in a waterproof jacket with a look on her face that said she'd rather have been somewhere else.

'Who's got the first-aid kit?' Reece asked, and there was general laughter.

'I have,' Alexa told him, joining in, 'and let anyone dare harm themselves. I'm off duty.'

Hazel eyes were meeting his, bright and challenging, and the message in them had nothing to do with first aid. She wanted to ask him what was going on and to say, 'You said I was pushy, but compared to your friend Natalie I'm a shrinking violet.'

But would she get the chance? There was never time to talk. Or at least that was how it seemed. This morning they'd been on the go from the moment they'd arrived at the surgery and it was the same every weekday.

She was free in the evenings, but was he? It didn't look like it. And if that was the case maybe Reece saw it as a good thing. It was one way of keeping her at arm's length.

She would like to know what had brought Natalie into the surgery in such a state. From being just a name in his past, she was rapidly making her presence felt, and the annoying thing was that Reece didn't seem to mind.

Alexa was the last out of the building as she'd had to change her clothes. As she turned the key in the lock, Bryan, with map in hand, gave the command to move off.

As they left Keswick in the continuing drizzle he was at the head of the party, with Reece, who had found himself a stout staff, and a slightly more cheerful Rebecca just behind. Following them were the receptionists, practice manager and the cleaners, with the three nurses bringing up the rear.

Plodding on doggedly, they approached Portinscale and when they passed Craith House, Carol and Tom waved them on.

This is the story of my life with regard to Reece and I, Alexa was thinking, near yet apart. I saw more of him in those first few days after we met than I've done in weeks.

A couple of miles further on he turned, his dark eyes flicking over the others until they came to rest on her, and Alexa's heart began to beat faster.

There was something in his glance that was making the grey day seem less drab, and if it wasn't lifting the mist around them, it was helping to clear the clouds in her mind.

Why was she letting the Rebeccas and ex-fiancées of the world bother her when Reece was looking at her like that? There *was* chemistry between them. She hadn't imagined it.

But it wasn't her that he'd asked to share his house, or he spent his evenings with, was it? If he was just turning on the charm for today he was in for a disappointment.

She looked away, unaware that he'd moved to one side and was waiting until they drew level. When he fell into step beside her she turned towards him, startled, and he said in a low voice that was meant only for her ears, 'I'm suffering from a lack of your company. Is there anything in the first-aid box to cure that?'

'No,' she said flatly. 'It doesn't contain anything for self-inflicted ailments. You always know where to find me, so what's the problem?'

They'd left the Newlands Valley behind by this time and were on the ascent of Catbells. Not wanting to be over-heard, they fell back, away from the others.

'I know that I haven't been around much of late,' he said. 'Natalie is a very demanding person. She always was, but at the moment she really does need me.'

'Don't tell me that you still want to talk about the old days,' Alexa said tightly. 'Or is it the future that she's so wrapped up in and sees you as part of it?'

'So you remember that night by the lake when she first appeared?'

'Of course I remember. The moment she beckoned, you were gone.'

'I went with her because she'd broken into a special mo-ment and, knowing what she's like, I wanted to get her away from you before she spoilt anything else. The moment she had me to herself, out came all her problems. She's got breast cancer and isn't coping very well. I'm supporting her the best I can and hoping that when she has her next scan there will be good news.'

'So that's it,' Alexa breathed. 'Why didn't you tell me before? I've been so miserable.'

'Natalie is the kind of person who thinks of cancer as some kind of stigma. She made me promise not to discuss it with anyone and as she's now got me as her GP, I couldn't break a patient's confidentiality.'

'Yet you're doing it now?'

'That's because I told her this morning that I needed to explain to you why I'm with her such a lot.'

'And she agreed?'

'Yes, when she'd calmed down.'

They had stopped and were facing each other in the swirling grey shroud of the mist.

'So?' he asked softly. 'Are we friends again?'

'You know I want more than that, Reece,' she said quietly as the rain dripped off her chin.

'Yes, I do.' His voice was sombre. 'But there are other things to consider besides the attraction between us.'

'No, there aren't!' she cried. 'All that matters is how we feel.'

'You're only concerned about how *you* feel, Alexa. What about my feelings? You know what my life has been of recent years, and I can't expect you to want that sort of existence for yourself, so...'

As she opened her mouth to protest he shook his head.

'No more!' He glanced around him. 'We seem to have been left behind and Bryan has the map. If the mist gets any thicker we'll never find them.'

The mist did get thicker and as they moved upwards towards the distinctive ridged summit of Catbells they didn't come across the rest of the party. It was as if the folk from the practice had disappeared into oblivion.

When they called out to them their voices came back in a woolly echo, and they both wondered which would be the best course of action—to carry on, or turn back.

There wouldn't be much joy in doing either under the existing weather conditions, and when they left the roof of Catbells and came to the rougher terrain of Maiden Moor they trudged on in silence, trying to keep to the track but knowing that it wasn't going to be easy.

At last Reece said, 'This is crazy, Alexa. I don't think we should go on in these conditions without a map. We can't see a foot in front of us, so I suggest that we shelter until it clears.'

She nodded her agreement. He was right. It would be foolish to go on and, even though these were not ideal conditions, at least she would have him to herself for a while.

He was smiling and, taking her wet face between his big palms, he said, 'It's nice to discover that you'll do as you're told once in a while. You're too cherishable to be allowed to fall into a bog or suchlike.'

Alexa took a deep breath. So he did care. And if Reece had no plans for them to be lovers, she supposed that friendship was better than nothing.

He was pointing towards an overhanging outlet of rock that had reared up in the mist, and as they moved towards it for shelter she was ready to tell him so.

Until he took a sideways step on ground that wasn't there and went crashing down a steep drop. Alexa could hear him rolling and bumping as he fell and then there was silence.

'Reece!' she shrieked, afraid to move in case she did the same thing, but there was no reply.

Horror had her in its grip. How far had he fallen? Twenty feet? Thirty feet? More? Not that much more surely, taking into account the length of time before the awful silence.

He must have struck his head on something, she thought frantically, or have hurt his spine. Whatever it was, it seemed as if he might be unconscious. She daren't think of anything worse.

At that moment the mist lifted slightly and she saw him lying at the bottom of a steep hillside, so at least she knew where to aim for.

As she began to make her way carefully down the uneven surface, Alexa thought tearfully of how they'd all laughed about the first-aid box and how she'd told them that no one was allowed to get hurt.

And now Reece, of all people, had been injured because

the mist distorted distance and blanked out what lay around them.

As she crouched down beside him he groaned and then slowly opened his eyes.

'What happened?' he said muzzily. 'The fall knocked the wind out of me.'

'There was a steep drop at the side of us and you stepped over the edge,' she told him, weak with relief to find him alive and conscious.

His leg was beneath him, and as he tried to bring it forward his face twisted.

'I think my leg is broken, Alexa,' he told her calmly. 'I'm going to need a splint. Can you climb back up there and find the staff I was carrying.'

She got to her feet.

'Yes, but what then? How am I going to get you to the top?'

'One thing at a time,' he said evenly as he observed her white face. 'We'll worry about that once I've managed to make myself mobile.'

'We have the first-aid box, don't forget,' she reminded him, with tears still threatening.

'Yes, but it doesn't carry splints, does it?'

'No...unfortunately.'

'So we're going to have to improvise until I get to hospital.'

She nodded bleakly. At that moment hospital seemed a long way off and without further discussion she set off back up the mountainside.

The stick that Reece had been carrying was a straight branch from a fallen sapling, and it lay on the edge of the drop that he'd fallen over. Alexa grasped it quickly and set off back down the slippery slope.

He was lying with his eyes closed when she reached his side again but was still prepared to take charge.

'Stay as you are,' she told him firmly. 'I'm taking over.'

Snapping the stick to the right length, she made a make-shift splint and then looked around for something to secure it with.

'Tear my shirt into strips,' he said.

Alexa shook her head. 'You need to stay still. I would have to take your jacket off and then the shirt. You mustn't move until we've sorted the leg out.'

'So?'

'You're not the only one wearing a shirt.' Without more ado, she pulled off her waterproof coat and unbuttoned the cotton blouse she was wearing underneath.

If she hadn't been so overwrought at the mess they were in Alexa might have seen the funny side of the situation. She'd imagined herself one day undressing for Reece and them making love in some idyllic setting, and here she was, taking off her clothes and tearing them up to make a splint for a broken leg.

His face was grey by the time she'd got the leg in position. Eyeing him anxiously, she said, 'There's no way you're going to be able to get up to the top again. We need a stretcher and paramedics to carry you up. Have you got your mobile?'

'Yes, somewhere. It was in my jacket pocket but it's not there now.'

Two pieces of broken plastic were lying nearby with the inside of the phone tangled amongst them, so that line of communication had to be discarded.

'I'm going to get help,' Alexa told him. 'The mist will have to clear soon.'

'Oh, yes?' he questioned dubiously. 'Who says so?'

'I do,' she said, managing a smile.

'Yes, well, you're not putting yourself at risk on my account,' he told her decisively. 'I've been in worse situations than this many a time, but have never been lucky

enough to have such special company. I can't think of anyone I'd rather be with if I'm going to break my leg.'

He was something else, she thought. It went without saying that he was in a lot of pain and here he was, making
jokes. Her eyes filled with tears. She loved him and all he
wanted from her was friendship.

The grey blanket of the mist was still hovering and even
though she was desperate to get help, Alexa knew if she
left Reece she mightn't be able to find him again as she
wasn't sure where she was.

He'd closed his eyes again and unable to help herself,
Alexa put her lips to his damp brow and said softly, 'I've
got a cold drink in my rucksack and a supply of painkill-
ers.'

His skin felt cold and she wondered if the flask of hot
soup that was also part of her provisions would be a better
idea.

'Or how about some minestrone soup with the tablets?'
she suggested, with a feeling that he might be in shock
after the fracture and she hadn't got any hot sweet tea to
offer.

'Can't have the soup,' he murmured. 'I need an empty
stomach in case I have to go to Theatre when I get to
hospital.' And then, to her delight, he went on, 'But having
you kiss my brow again or giving me a cuddle, would be
most acceptable.'

She'd been aching to hold him and, taking him carefully
in her arms, Alexa kissed his brow, his closed eyes, the
strong stem of his throat, everything but his lips. Those she
would kiss when they were offered freely.

When she lifted her head a shaft of sunlight was cutting
through the mist and her heart lifted. She didn't want to
leave him, but lying there on the wet grass wasn't going to
do Reece any good and the fracture needed urgent attention.

'Reece, darling,' she said softly, 'I'm going to get help.

The mist is clearing.' She gave a watery smile. 'Don't run away while I'm gone, will you?'

When she'd climbed back to the top of ridge again she stood, undecided. Should she go forward in the hope of finding the others, or go back to Keswick to get help?

If the mist continued to lift she wasn't likely to get lost, but it was the length of time that she would be away that was troubling her.

'Hello, there!' a voice said suddenly from nearby, and Alexa felt her legs go weak with relief.

'Be careful, Rebecca!' she cried. 'We're on the edge of a drop. Reece is down there with what appears to be a broken leg. I was just setting off to get help!'

'It's a good job I was coming back this way, then,' Rebecca said in her usual clipped tones. 'I had a call on my mobile to say that my car has been stolen and I decided to turn back. You'd better take me to him, Alexa.'

'Rebecca!' Reece exclaimed when the two women appeared beside him. 'You're a welcome sight!'

She smiled and Alexa turned away, but the characterless doctor was about to bestow what for her was rare praise.

'Well done with the splint, Alexa.'

Reece was showing signs of trying to heave himself upright but Rebecca shook her head.

'I'm going back up to the top to phone Mountain Rescue,' she told him. 'Reception will be better up there.'

When she'd gone Reece asked, 'What made Rebecca come looking for us?'

'She didn't. Someone phoned her to say that her car's been stolen and she was going back to sort it out.'

'Lucky for us,' he said, taking her hand in his. 'I was worried sick about you going off into the mist on your own.'

'And how do you think I felt...leaving you in this state?'

He managed a smile. 'So we're agreed that we've both been spared a lot of anxiety?'

'Yes,' she said huskily. 'And all I want now is to see you safely out of here and getting treatment.'

'Bless you, Alexa,' he said softly, and for a moment the trauma of the situation was forgotten. The only thing they were aware of was their need of each other.

Reece was about to capitulate on this rain-swept mountainside. He was going to admit that he loved her as much as she loved him. Alexa could feel it in her bones.

It wasn't the most romantic of settings, both of them huddled in waterproof jackets, with mud-soaked boots on their feet and Reece obviously in a lot of pain with his makeshift splint. But none of that was registering.

'It's sorted,' Rebecca called from up above. 'Mountain Rescue are on their way.' Then she was slithering back down towards them and the moment was gone.

It was midnight when Alexa got back to Craith House. Reece had been taken to hospital, X-rayed and found to have a fractured tibia.

Fortunately it was a straightforward break. There was no realignment of the bone ends to be done. But even so they were keeping him in overnight for observation.

Rebecca had left them to it, her stolen car being uppermost thought in her mind. It had been Alexa who had stayed until he'd had his leg put in plaster and been bedded in a small side ward.

'Go home, Alexa,' he'd said the moment they'd been alone. 'You've had a dreadful day and must be exhausted.'

'And what about you?' she'd said softly. 'Yours hasn't exactly been a picnic.'

He'd given a tired grin. 'I'm not going to argue with that, but it hasn't all been broken bones and wet mist. I've had you by my side.'

'That's what friends are for,' she'd said brightly, hoping that he'd take her up on it. But he'd made no comment, just eyed her consideringly, and she'd told herself that it didn't matter.

As long as Reece was safe and not hurt any worse than they'd thought, she'd felt able to gather up her damp belongings and leave him to the care of the nursing staff before exhaustion claimed her.

CHAPTER SEVEN

AND now here she was, back in her own small sanctum, tired, bedraggled and thinking that it seemed a lifetime since Carol and Tom had waved them past Craith House that morning.

Sleep was tugging at Alexa, but so was the balm of a shower, and as she stood in slender nakedness beneath it her mind went back to those moments on the mountainside with Reece.

It had been a time of great anxiety, but there had been a pleasurable side to it as well. The chance to hold and comfort him had presented itself and there was no way she would have wanted to miss out on that.

Without the assistance of Rebecca they might still have been up there, and as she towelled herself dry she wondered if she should ring to ask if her car had turned up.

'Yes, it did,' Rebecca said when Alexa followed up the thought. 'It had been dumped when it ran out of petrol, but fortunately it wasn't damaged. In fact, I've just driven to see Reece in it. I got there just after you'd left.'

'And was he all right?'

'Yes, and delighted to see me. He said that my appearance out there on the mountain was magical.'

'It was,' Alexa agreed flatly.

There was no mention of her own part in the incident. While she'd been dreaming about the precious moments they'd shared, Reece had been rapturising about Rebecca making a phone call.

'I'm glad you've got your car back,' she said, stifling a

yawn. 'It's been a long day so I'll wish you good-night, Rebecca.'

'And so where did *you* get to on Saturday?' Beryl asked when they met in the nurse's room on Monday morning.

'We got left behind and Reece fell and broke his leg,' Alexa told her friend.

'I don't believe it!' she exclaimed. 'I've just heard him call in his first patient.'

Alexa goggled at her.

'What? He can't have. They kept him in hospital over-night on Saturday and he was being "nursed" by Rebecca yesterday.'

Beryl shrugged.

'Maybe so, but it doesn't alter the fact that he's here now.'

Having no alternative but to accept the fact, Alexa gazed into space. She was the one who'd been with him at the time of the accident, but she hadn't got a look in since. Rebecca had taken over.

She'd gone to the hospital as soon as she'd got her car back late on Saturday night, and when she, Alexa, had rung the hospital on Sunday morning to ask how Reece was and if she could take him home, she'd been told that he'd already left with Dr Soames.

A phone call from him later in the morning had been to the effect that Rebecca had insisted that he spend the day at her house and that she was going to transport him to his own some time during the evening.

'I think that it's her own welfare that Rebecca is thinking of as well as mine,' he'd said at the end of a stilted conversation. 'She has a lot on her mind and is desperate for company.' As if realising that bit of information was going down like a lead balloon, he'd finished with, 'I'll see you soon, Alexa.'

'Yes,' she'd said coolly. 'It's nice to know that you both have each other's welfare so much at heart.'

If he'd had anything to say to that he hadn't had a chance. She'd gone off the line.

So much for their togetherness, she'd thought as the day had stretched ahead emptily. She must have imagined it.

It was the middle of the morning and, aware that his mishap was the general topic of conversation, Reece decided that if Alexa wasn't going to come to him, he would have to go to her.

He'd been expecting her to come breezing in all morning and couldn't wait any longer for a glimpse of her. He knew she'd have liked to have brought him home from the hospital. That had been what he'd wanted, too, but Rebecca had appeared at his bedside soon after the surgeon had told him he could go home, and she'd been so insistent that he'd found it difficult to refuse her offer of a lift and subsequent hospitality.

It seemed that she'd rung to ask how he was and on being told he was about to be discharged, had gone straight to the hospital to offer transport.

She'd also insisted that she take him to her place so that she could look after him. Much as he'd have liked to assure her that he was quite capable of looking after himself, she'd offered in such a way that he hadn't been able to refuse, when all the time his mind had been on Alexa.

Back in his own bed, he'd had a restless night. His leg had been painful and every time he'd dozed off he'd dreamt that he and Alexa were back on the mountain.

He'd felt her soft lips on his brow, her arms holding him protectively, and each time he'd awakened he'd felt sick with disappointment.

But it was nothing to the disappointment he was experiencing now. She was only feet away and yet he felt that she was just as out of reach as in his dreams.

Alexa was filling in the notes of a patient who'd just been treated in the nurse's room when the door opened and Reece stood there, balancing on crutches.

'I'd heard that you were here,' she said before he could get a word in. 'How are you feeling?'

Dark eyes were observing her thoughtfully. 'Better, thank you. But are you really interested? You haven't exactly been falling over yourself to find out.'

Shame filled her. He was right. She'd let pique blot out her feelings for him.

'I was annoyed that you didn't ask me to pick you up from the hospital. When I rang there yesterday you were already in Rebecca's clutches,' she told him with reluctant candour.

His laugh was mirthless.

'An apt description. But as she arrived only minutes after I'd been told I could go, it was difficult to refuse her offer when all the time I wanted to be with you.'

'So that's how it was,' she said with a conciliatory smile, and then with a change of subject so that her capitulation shouldn't be seen as too complete, she asked, 'Should you be here so soon after the accident?'

'Why not? I'll be seated most of the day, and as you're so desperate to assist with my mobility perhaps you'd like to drive me home.'

'Of course,' she agreed immediately, still a little contrite but bouncing back nevertheless. 'It will be a pleasure. But as my car isn't as big as yours, you might have to stick the leg you can't bend out of the window.'

He laughed and Alexa was relieved that they'd made their peace again. Leaning on his crutches in the doorway he looked so agreeable and wholesome it was all she could do not to throw herself into his arms. But for one thing they weren't free. They were keeping the crutches in place.

'So, I'll see you when we've finished for the day,' he was saying, 'and I might as well go straight to Craith House to eat. OK?'

Alexa nodded, her good humour back in full force. 'Yes, and then I'll run you home when you're ready.'

Suddenly he was grave.

'I don't know how I'm going to exist without you when I leave here, Alexa.'

'You don't *have* to go,' she said carefully. 'Surely you can please yourself.'

He observed her without speaking and she thought she saw indecision in his eyes, but that wasn't Reece, was it? He was the most decisive person she'd ever met.

She'd thrown out a challenge, though, and now she was wishing she hadn't. If Reece ever gave in to the attraction between them it would have to be of his own choosing, not because she'd wheedled round him.

If he did have a reply for her it wasn't forthcoming. A familiar voice outside in the passage indicated that John was visiting and it was the only time she could ever remember not being pleased to see him.

Reece was swivelling round on his crutches, his face brightening at the sound of his friend's voice. With a cheery wave in her direction from the former head of the practice, the two men moved off towards Reece's consulting room.

'So what's all this, then?' the elderly GP asked when they'd seated themselves.

'Don't mention it!' Reece said with a wry grimace. 'I've been in all sorts of situations and never come to grief. Then here, on my own territory, I go and break my leg.'

'How did it happen?'

'On Saturday everyone from the practice went on a sponsored walk and Alexa and I got cut off from the others in a heavy mist.'

'Oh, aye?'

'Don't read anything into it that isn't there, John,' Reece warned him with a mirthless laugh. 'I fell over the edge of a steep drop and fractured my tibia.'

'And that's it?'

'Yes.'

'You didn't enjoy being marooned in the mist with my favourite practice nurse?'

'Of course I did,' he groaned. 'She's an amazing woman. Alexa was anxious, loving and tender, all rolled into one, but I can't put a blight on her life by allowing her to become attached to someone like me.'

'They don't come any better,' John grunted. 'There's nothing I'd like better than to see the two of you make a go of it.'

The door was open and outside in the passage Alexa had heard his comment. With her arms full of medical supplies from the storeroom she became still as she waited for Reece's reply, but when it came there was no joy in it.

'Don't get your hopes up,' he told his friend, and as she moved slowly towards her own domain with dragging feet and a heavy heart, Robbie Durkin loomed up in front of her.

'Hi, there, Lexy,' he said breezily. 'How's things?'

'Could be better,' she told him listlessly.

'So how about us getting together again? I promise I'll not take you anywhere you don't want to go.'

She managed to drag up a smile from somewhere.

'I'll think about it, but not now, Robbie.'

'OK. I'll be in touch later in the week, then?'

She nodded, and as a patient waiting outside her room eyed her hopefully, she said, 'Come in, Mr Jarvis.' Once he'd obeyed she asked, 'How's the discomfort at the moment?'

'Bad…Nurse,' he said grimly. 'I've never had stomach-ache like it. Dr Lomas says I'm to have some tests done as it may be irritable bowel syndrome.'

Alexa glanced at his notes.

'Yes, so I see. If that should be the case there's medication you can take, but Doctor won't be able to prescribe it until we know for sure.'

'Supposing it's cancer.'

Her smile flashed out and this time it wasn't a grimace. It was the kind, reassuring beam she had for those who were frightened or worried.

'Let's not cross our bridges too soon, Mr Jarvis. Wait and see, eh?'

He sighed, and they both knew that his fears weren't exactly groundless.

During the long afternoon that followed the blighting of her hopes, Alexa decided that she'd had enough of being kept on the sidelines of Reece's life.

From now on it would be he who did the running, if any. She was going to get on with her life and he could get on with his. As it seemed like a case of 'never the twain shall meet', there was no point in her languishing after him.

When he came hobbling out onto the forecourt at six o'clock he eyed her warily and she thought, You have need to be wary of me from now on, my love, as we are about to move into different hemispheres, and if you don't believe me, just watch!

'So how has the day been?' he asked as he manoeuvred himself into the passenger seat of her Escort.

'Revealing.'

'In what way?'

'What was it that you once said to me? It was for you

to know and me to find out. Turn it around and you've got your answer.'

They were heading towards Portinscale and as fields appeared on either side of the road Reece said, 'Don't let's fight, Alexa.'

'No one's fighting. It's just that I've seen the light and am no longer dazzled.'

'I suppose that cryptic remark has to mean something,' he said good-humouredly with a glance at her set face. 'Puzzle time, is it?'

They were pulling up in front of Craith House and Alexa didn't answer. Instead she went round to his side of the car and opened the door.

'Do you need any help?' she asked woodenly.

'No, thanks. I can manage,' he told her smoothly, and on that note of confidence she left him and made her way to her own apartment.

Once she'd eaten Alexa awaited the call from the house to drive Reece home, but time kept passing and it didn't come. It seemed that he was in no hurry to get to his ramshackle farmhouse and she wondered what he was doing inside Carol's place.

Eventually she went to find him, knowing she wouldn't be able to settle down until she'd seen him safely home.

She had to pass through the guest-house kitchen and what she saw there made her heart miss a beat. Carol was slumped on a chair, as white as a sheet, and sipping at a glass of water, with Tom and Reece hovering beside her.

'What's wrong with Carol?' she cried, hurrying to her sister's side.

'She fainted,' Tom said raggedly, 'and I called Reece out of the dining room to attend to her.'

'What is it, Caro?' Alexa asked gently, taking her sister's limp hand in hers. 'This isn't like you. I don't think I've ever seen you in this state before.'

'That's because I've never been pregnant before,' Carol said shakily. 'I've just had a chat with Reece and we think that there's a strong possibility that I might be.'

Alexa's mouth was a round 'O' of delight.

'I'm going to have a niece or nephew!' she whooped.

'I won't be certain until I've been tested, but I'm pretty sure,' Carol said as the colour began to creep back into her face. Taking Tom's hand in hers, she looked up into his anxious face. 'Don't worry, darling. It was just a faint.'

Reece was observing them smilingly.

'Come into the surgery tomorrow and we'll find out for sure. Unless you'd rather go to the chemist.'

She shook her head.

'No. I'd rather see you, Reece. When you first came here I told Alexa that I was looking forward to my next ailment if you were going to be one of the doctors at the practice, but I never dreamt that it might be this.' She squeezed her husband's hand more tightly. 'We might be going to have a baby, Tom. Isn't it wonderful?'

He didn't answer. There was no need. The joy on his face was enough.

'So you're happy about that?' Reece questioned as Alexa drove him to his rented house.

Alexa was conscious that she was still smiling.

'Yes! Just as long as you think that Carol is pregnant.'

'Obviously I can't be sure,' he said, 'but from what she tells me, all the signs are there. Morning sickness, tender breasts, and she's actually missed a couple of periods. Did you not know?'

Alexa shook her long chestnut locks. 'No. She's had one or two false alarms over the last couple of years and she vowed that the next time she wasn't going to say anything to anyone until she was sure. I've thought that she looked a bit peaky of late, but I'm afraid I've been rather selfishly wrapped up in my own affairs.'

'With regard to that, I've had your friend Robbie Durkin in to see me today.'

'Robbie is not part of my affairs, Reece. You know that very well. But if *you're* going to put me back on the shelf, he might come knocking.'

'Now you're being ridiculous. What's brought all this on?'

'You have.'

'Me?'

'Yes, and don't ask me what I mean. The subject is closed.'

They were at the farm by this time and as Reece got slowly out of the car, grasping his crutches, she just couldn't leave him without making sure he could manage.

'Can I make you a drink or anything before I go?' she asked stiffly. 'Or would you like me to make up a bed for you downstairs?'

No, thanks. I can manage all right. If need be, I'll ascend the stairs rear end first...and I do know how to switch the kettle on.'

'Clever clogs!'

He ignored the sarcasm and to her surprise said, 'You can stay and keep me company for a while if you like.'

She was tempted but told him, 'No, thanks. If you're quite sure that you don't need me for anything else, I'll be on my way.'

He swung himself in front of her on the crutches, blocking the doorway.

'What's the matter, Alexa?' he asked. 'You weren't in such a rush to leave me on that cold mountainside. You were fantastic.'

'Huh! Fantastic, was I? So much so that you're still trying to fob me off onto Robbie.'

He was deadly serious now.

'Maybe I don't want to believe my luck.'

'Try to believe this, then.'

Taking advantage of his immobility, she placed her arms around him and covered his mouth with hers. Then, letting out all her pent-up feelings, she kissed him long and lingeringly.

'Whew!' he exclaimed when she let him go.

'Exactly.' She touched him gently on the cheek. 'Goodnight, Reece. Sleep well.' And with a swirl of her skirts she was gone.

Carol *was* pregnant. When she came out of Reece's consulting room the next day she was radiant, and the two sisters hugged each other delightedly.

'You must get more help at Craith House,' Alexa said when they'd calmed down.

'Yes, all right. I will,' Carol agreed. 'I can't wait to get home to tell Tom the good news. He couldn't come with me because we're expecting some new arrivals.'

For the rest of the day Alexa was walking on air, and if there was just the slightest tinge of envy buried somewhere deep inside her she told herself that it was only natural.

Carol and Tom had a secure, loving marriage and now they were going to be blessed with a family. Would that state of affairs ever come her way?

She knew without doubt that she'd found the man that she wanted to spend the rest of her life with, to have children with, but would he ever see *her* in that light?

Reece was clever and caring, strong and resilient. Resilient enough to resist her? He'd responded to her impulsive kiss like a man with fire in his loins, but was that enough?

If it wasn't, in years to come she could see herself in the role of maiden aunt to Carol's child.

*   *   *

Jessica Thomas was on warfarin for a replacement heart valve, and she came in to see the nurses once a month to have her blood checked.

The valve had been in place for almost thirty years and until she'd recently seen the consultant who'd performed the operation all that time ago, Jessica had been dreading having to have a new valve fitted on the grounds of wear and tear.

But to her relief he'd told her that it would last her lifetime, as long as her blood levels were checked regularly and she never forgot to take her medication.

A competent senior citizen, she had always gone to the blood clinic at the hospital previously, but of recent months the system had changed and she had been referred to her local practice for the monthly blood check.

If there was any problem the surgery would get back to her when the result came through, and after years of long practice Jessica would adjust the warfarin dosage accordingly.

'And how are you today, Mrs Thomas?' Alexa asked when the task was completed.

'Fine' was the brisk reply. 'Just as long as my blood isn't like treacle, or alternatively water, as it can change almost from minute to minute.'

'We'll phone you as soon as the result comes through,' Alexa told her reassuringly, and as Jessica Thomas bustled off to whatever other pursuits the day held for her, she called in the next patient.

'Robbie!' she exclaimed. 'What are *you* doing here?'

He was looking decidedly uncomfortable.

'Dr Rowlinson wants me to have a urine test.'

'Why?'

'I'm not sure. Kidneys maybe...or bladder. I've been having problems.'

As she passed him a plastic cup Alexa hid a smile. The

process he was about to embark on didn't fit in very well with his macho image.

'First door on the right,' she called as he scuttled out, holding the plastic container as inconspicuously as possible.

'So what's with Robbie?' she asked when Reece appeared at the end of surgery.

'Don't know until we get the sample back. There was a trace of blood in it. Might be a cyst in the bladder.'

'I see.'

'Don't worry too much, Alexa. I'll look after him.'

'I'm not worrying about him any more than I would any other patient,' she told him levelly. 'You don't need to give him the VIP treatment on my account.'

'I hope that you're not suggesting that I give some patients more attention than others,' he said in chilly tones. 'You should know me better than that.'

'Really? The more I see of you, the more I realise that I don't know you at all.'

'Is that so? Then maybe it's perhaps as well,' he retorted with the chill persisting. 'And by the way, I've got a lift home. Rebecca is taking some of her stuff to the house, but she's going to dine with me at Craith House first.'

His face had softened.

'Good news about Carol's pregnancy, isn't it?'

Alexa's face brightened in spite of what he'd just said. 'Yes. I'm so thrilled for them.'

'Are you envious, Alexa?' he asked gravely.

She could feel her colour rising but the truth never hurt anyone.

'Yes,' she told him flatly. 'I am a bit, but I'm dealing with it.' Without giving him the chance to say more, she went out to the car park and got into her car.

*   *   *

As the golden summer drew to a close the weeks seemed to take on a pattern, with Reece and Rebecca now living in the same house and Alexa once again on a friendly footing with Robbie Durkin. Though the interest was mostly on his part.

With Rebecca always on hand to provide transport, and Reece taking care that he and Alexa had no time for anything personal during working hours, she was getting the message.

She often wished she could turn back the clock to when they'd first met, so that they could start all over again, but would it have worked out any differently?

Alexa was what she was. Impulsive, passionate and vulnerable. While Reece, who was equally aware of the chemistry between them, was strong and implacable.

Sometimes she found him observing her with a strange expression, but he never offered to tell her what was in his mind and there was no way she was going to ask.

The calendar on her wall said that the weeks were flying past, and every time she thought about Reece going back to the kind of life he'd had before returning to the Lakes, it was as if a black cloud had settled upon her.

All of that was the downside of her life. The upside was seeing the precious bump that a radiant Carol was carrying in front of her and watching Tom's protective tenderness towards her sister.

Reece had asked her if she was envious of them and she'd admitted that she was. Would she ever carry the child of the man she adored? It was doubtful.

John Hendrix came in early one morning and when Alexa eyed him in surprise he said, 'I'm here to take Reece to hospital. He's hoping they'll remove the plaster cast today.'

'Oh, I see,' she said awkwardly.

He was observing her from beneath bushy brows.

'Hasn't he told you? I thought that you and he were...'

Her smile was wry. '"Were" describes it exactly. Reece has his life mapped out and I don't come into it.'

The elderly doctor was frowning.

'I'm afraid that he has good reason to be wary. Reece had a bad experience with the Bracknell woman. So much so that I thought he would never get involved with anyone again. But I sense a change in him since he met you. His defences are cracking because he's met someone very special. I've seen the way he looks at you.'

'You mean as if he's thinking, Oh, dear! What shall we do about Alexa?'

'No. As if he's in love with you.'

She gave a careless shrug.

'If anything, Reece is in love with his job, John.'

'It certainly means a lot to him, Alexa. More than you and I can ever know. We would have to have been out there with him to appreciate the amount of satisfaction that comes from giving that kind of service, but there's more to life than work.'

'Try telling him that,' she murmured.

At that moment the man in question came out of his room and John got to his feet.

'I hope that all goes well at the hospital,' she said coolly as Reece looked at them questioningly. Skirting round them, she went into her own domain and closed the door behind her with a decisive click.

They were back within the hour and Reece's smile said that the plaster cast had gone.

'How about helping me celebrate after evening surgery?' he suggested to the staff, and within minutes plans had been made for all those who were available to congregate at a nearby wine bar.

Perversely Alexa hadn't said whether she intended being there or not. All the time he'd been at the hospital she'd been thinking about the grey afternoon when the accident had happened.

It had been an anxious time and yet out there on the rain-swept mountain they'd been so close, so in tune. It had been the same right up to the time they'd admitted Reece to hospital, but afterwards he'd seemed happy to let Rebecca take over.

'So are you joining us or not?' Reece asked as she cleared away at the end of the day.

'I suppose so,' she said flatly.

He tutted.

'There's no need to force yourself, Alexa. What's the matter? Have you made plans to meet Durkin?'

'No.'

'Then in that case there's nothing to stop you coming, and you of all people should be there. You were there for me that day on the mountain. My rock and shield.'

Suddenly her apathy went and she was in fighting mood.

'And that's how I want it to be...always,' she cried. 'You and I there for each other. I'm not the one responsible for the great divide!'

She could see that she was wasting her time. His expression said that there wasn't going to be a joyful moment of mutual understanding.

'Let's just stick to tonight's arrangements,' he said tightly. 'We're only talking about a quick get-together. Surely you can spare the time.'

The fire in her bones had gone as quickly as it came.

'Yes, I suppose so,' she said flatly. 'I'll see you there.' She looked down at her neat blue uniform. 'It will be like this, I'm afraid. I haven't anything with me to change into.'

He was smiling now.

'What you're wearing doesn't matter. Just bring yourself, Alexa.'

He couldn't tell her that she wasn't the only one who

was aware of the weeks flying past. If he left the Lakes he would be leaving his heart behind.

He knew that he was acting like a fool. In the short time that was left he should be grasping every opportunity to spend some prime time with her, but instead he was keeping her at a distance.

It mattered that she should be there with them tonight, though, and they would be safe with the rest of the crowd. He wouldn't be falling into a pit of his own making.

It was the first get-together of the practice staff since the ill-fated sponsored walk, and when Alexa arrived she found them drinking and chatting amicably around a large table in a corner of the bar.

Reece got to his feet the moment he saw her and Rebecca, who'd been sitting next to him, fixed her with her cold blue gaze.

'There's room here, Alexa,' Beryl called across, as if she'd read her mind, and with a grateful smile Alexa went to join the other nurses.

They were all drinking champagne, and when he'd filled her glass Reece went back to his seat next to Rebecca. Alexa was conscious that his eyes were on herself, even though he was listening to what the blonde doctor was saying.

By eight o'clock most of the staff were making tracks for home and Alexa intended being with them. This kind of gathering was torture. Being in Reece's company and yet so far apart. During the day it didn't affect her so much as they both had a job to do, but this was different.

She was surprised to see that Rebecca was one of the first to leave, so it would seem that she wasn't driving Reece home tonight, Alexa thought. He wouldn't have his car with him as he hadn't known earlier in the day whether the cast on his leg would be removed.

He could always get a taxi, she supposed, but it would

be rude not to offer a lift when she was going in the same direction.

They were the only two left by the time he'd settled the bar bill, and as he turned towards her Alexa said, 'I see that Rebecca has already gone. Can I give you a lift home?'

'Yes, please. If you're sure it's no trouble.'

She shook her head. How could he think it would be a trouble? The aloof attitude she'd been adopting was tearing her apart. The chance to be with him, if only for a short time, was too tempting to pass by.

As they went to her car Reece said, 'It's great to have the cast off my leg but, having walked with it in one position for so long, would you say that physiotherapy is called for, Nurse?'

'I would indeed…Doctor,' she replied, and they both ended up laughing.

The relaxed moment came to an end when, unable to contain her curiosity, Alexa asked, 'Where was Rebecca rushing off to in such haste?'

He pursed his lips as if doubtful whether he should answer her question, and she said into the silence, 'It's some sort of big secret, is it?'

'No. Not exactly. It's just that if nothing comes of it I feel that she won't want anyone at the practice to know.'

'Know what?'

'That she's gone to meet the man she used to be engaged to. He wants a reconciliation, but she's not sure how it will turn out.'

'So the fact that she's been happier of late has nothing to do with you!' Alexa exclaimed in slow surprise.

'No! Of course not. I'm not attracted to cold women.'

'Yes, but that doesn't stop them from being attracted to you.'

He was fastening his seat belt and when he looked up their eyes were level in the small confines of the car.

'Maybe, but that isn't my problem, is it? My problem, Alexa, is you.'

'You're saying that you wish we'd never met?'

'Yes! No! Of course not! But I have to admit that you've complicated my life.'

'I'm sorry about that.'

His smile was wry.

'No, you're not. Admit it.'

'All right, then, I'm not sorry. I know what I want, which is more than you seem to do.'

'Oh, I know what I want, have no doubts on that score. But I haven't got such an uncomplicated mind as you. I think things out before I act.'

'And I don't?'

'No, you don't.'

Alexa sighed. If there had been harmony between them she wouldn't have wanted the mellow autumn evening to end, but they were going round in circles again.

'I think it's time to call it a day until we have something relevant to say to each other,' she told him flatly, and when they pulled up in front of his house she bade him a brief farewell and drove off.

CHAPTER EIGHT

OCTOBER had come, with a chill wind lifting the fallen leaves, and Alexa's thoughts kept going back to the golden evenings she'd spent by the lake with Reece. It seemed an eternity ago. Almost as if it had been in another life.

They were heading nowhere, she told herself at the end of each day where they'd worked amicably enough together and then gone their separate ways at the end of it.

The town was less busy with the changing seasons, but it didn't seem to diminish the number of those waiting to be seen at the surgery.

If her social life was as busy as her work schedule, she would have nothing to complain about, Alexa thought frequently. But it wasn't, and unless she was prepared to spend all her free time with Robbie it wasn't going to improve.

It was clear that Reece had taken note of her abrupt ultimatum on the night she'd driven him home after his cast removal.

She'd suggested that they keep away from each other until such time as they had something of real interest to discuss, and so far it would appear that they hadn't.

But she still found his dark, enigmatic gaze on her when he thought she wasn't looking and there were times when she thought he looked tired and low-spirited, but she told herself that the ball was in his court.

What Reece did when he was away from the practice she didn't know. Whatever it was it certainly didn't involve her.

Maybe he called to see John, or went to the lakeside theatre, she thought. Or went to offer support to Natalie

Bracknell. Though there had been no signs of him taking the road to Buttermere of late.

Logic said that feeling as he did about the way his ex-fiancée had deceived him, there wasn't likely to be a resurgence of *that* dead passion. Just as it looked as if there wasn't going to be anything onward-going in their own relationship.

Carol had been almost three months pregnant that night she'd fainted, and now she was looking forward to a December birth.

It was going to be a time of arrivals and departures, Alexa told herself. She hoped the coming of her new nephew or niece would help to take away the pain of Reece going.

On a night when she was last out of the surgery, Alexa found that her car wouldn't start. It had been out on the parking lot all day and it seemed as if the battery was flat.

She was feeling tired and edgy and as she stood there in the quickening dark the effort of going to get the bus or phoning for a taxi seemed just too much. As she stood eyeing the car frustratedly there was the sound of another vehicle approaching, and to her surprise Reece's car pulled up beside her.

She'd been even more aware of him than usual during that day. The long, lean efficiency of him. His dark pelt of hair and thoughtful, brown glance. The hands that had made her melt at their touch. They had all been invading her senses and now, incredibly, he was there beside her.

He rolled down the window.

'What's wrong?' he asked.

'I think that the battery is flat.'

'It's fortunate that I came back, then, isn't it? Hop in.'

'Why *did* you come back?' Alexa asked as she slid into the passenger seat.

'We need to talk.'

'Huh! How did you know I would be there?'

'Because you were still busy when I left, so I took the chance and turned the car round.'

'It's a bit sudden, isn't it? This desire to talk.'

'Not really,' he said levelly, and she subsided into silence until they were almost in Portinscale.

'So where are we going to have this long overdue chat?' Alexa said coolly when he pulled up at the front of Craith House.

'You could invite me in for a coffee.'

Her eyes widened.

'My place?'

'Why not?'

She must be dreaming. After weeks of silence Reece wanted to talk. What had brought this about?

'Yes, all right, then,' she agreed.

He couldn't go on like this, Reece thought as they skirted the guest house to get to her garden flat in the chilly October night. He was crazy to think of leaving Alexa.

Her name thundered in his ears with every heartbeat. His mind was full of her. She was playing havoc with his senses.

He'd said that they needed to talk and she hadn't exactly fallen over herself with excitement at the prospect. But she didn't yet know that once again he was going to alter his plans for the woman he loved.

During the ride back from Keswick the ache inside him had been so strong he'd had to fight the urge to pull to the side of the road and take her in his arms.

But he knew that Alexa had changed. When they'd first met she'd been confident, bouncy and very beautiful. She still was beautiful, incredibly so, but some of the confidence and bounce had gone and he felt that he was to blame.

He'd seen her with Robbie Durkin several times and

she'd looked happy enough, so maybe he was rating his place in her affections too high. Perhaps she was changing her mind about him and it would serve him right if she was.

'Nice,' he said as he looked around him at the inside of her small apartment.

The rooms were like their owner, clean and uncluttered. They were painted in bright sunshine colours, with scatter rugs on polished floors and modern furniture with simple lines.

Alexa was filling the kettle and she looked round at the compliment.

'It suits me.'

'Yes, I'm sure it does,' he agreed as she turned back to the tap.

She kept her hair tied back during working hours and his eyes were on the soft skin at the back of her neck. He wanted to press his lips to it and slide his arms around her slender waist inside the crisp cotton uniform.

In that moment all other thoughts went out of his mind and he found himself moving towards her with the longing that never went increasing by the second.

Sensing that he was approaching, Alexa swung round and found herself close up against his chest.

'I'm desperate to hold you, Alexa,' he said softly as hazel eyes, wide and watchful, looked into his. 'These last weeks have been torture.'

'I'm not dressed for seduction,' she breathed, looking down at the black stockings and flat working shoes that went with her uniform.

Reece wasn't listening. He was putting self-denial to one side, and as he began to kiss her Alexa thought weakly that she wasn't 'undressed' for it either.

But that changed when, like two people in a trance, they went into her bedroom and Reece removed her clothes with a slow and tender reverence that made her weak with long-ing.

'I thought we'd come here to talk,' she reminded him unsteadily.

'Mmm…we have,' he murmured against her lips. 'Later, though.'

His touch was a spark to her desire, his nakedness breath-taking. They were both consumed with their need for each other. They had fasted too long, Alexa thought breathlessly as she realised the extent of Reece's arousal.

This was the moment she'd dreamed of, but where had it come from? She hadn't expected tonight to be any dif-ferent from any other.

He'd said that they needed to talk, but their voices were silent. Body language had taken over. Its message was there between his lean flanks and in the taut globes of her breasts.

As they came together triumphant joy washed over her. At last Reece was admitting that they belonged, she told herself dreamily when the climax was over and they lay in sated languor in each other's arms. She would remember this day for the rest of her life.

She'd discovered that this man didn't spread his affec-tions around carelessly. For him to have given in to such longing could mean only one thing. He *did* love her. He *did* want her.

Reece was raising himself up onto one elbow, and as he looked down on her he was wishing that they had talked first…that he'd told her what was in his mind, instead of making love to her the moment they'd got inside.

Alexa would see it as him taking her for granted. That now he was ready to make the grand gesture there was no reason why they shouldn't make love. He'd kept her dan-gling for weeks, and now—as part of the package—he wanted sex. The elation was leaving him. The tide of passion that they'd been swept along on was receding, and he knew that she saw it in his eyes.

'I'm sorry, Alexa. I lost control,' he said quietly. 'We should have talked first. But having had so little personal contact with you of late, and then being so close to you in the car, my longing for you blotted out every other thought.'

She was out of his reach and on her feet almost before he'd finished speaking, her face drained of colour as sick disappointment hit her.

'What are you saying?' she cried. 'That you're still going, but feel you should have mentioned it again before we made love...just so that I didn't get any wrong ideas?'

He shook his head.

'I invited myself in here to tell you what has been on my mind for days and had no intention of getting carried away like I did before we'd had the chance to talk.'

'So I was just a quick lay, was I? Is that what you're saying?' she choked. 'You had a rush of testosterone and decided to offload it onto me before once more hammering home your intentions.'

His face was as white as her own.

'No! It wasn't like that. I respect you.'

'Respect! It looks like it. I'm good enough for making love to but not anything else. Next thing you'll be telling me you admire me, or hold me in the highest regard. There's one thing I can say about Robbie Durkin. I know where I am with him. He isn't picking me up and putting me down all the time.

'The sooner you carry on with your interrupted career the better. Maybe once you've gone my life will return to normal, and it can't come quickly enough.'

She'd been throwing on her clothes during the brief, angry altercation and now at her request he got slowly off the bed and began to do likewise.

Turning her back on him, she went into the kitchen and gazed blindly out of the window until his voice coming from the open doorway had her swinging round.

'I'm sorry, Alexa,' he said with a gravity that brought doom to every word. 'I'm totally ashamed that I let my feelings take over.'

'You're taking it out on me because of Natalie Bracknell, aren't you?' she cried. 'Making me pay for her misdeeds! Using the job as an excuse. The sooner you go the better! I can't wait.'

She turned back to the window, the set of her shoulders telling him how far apart they'd become in the last few minutes.

Reece was so full of sensible reasoning he left her at a loss for words, she thought angrily. But whatever kind of logic he was using, he was wrong. Totally wrong. They belonged together. The rest of the world could wait.

Yet she wasn't going to tell him so and seconds later she heard the outer door close behind him. It was then that she wept.

Alexa wasn't to know that twice Reece turned back with the desire in him to tell her that he wasn't going. But what was the point? he thought bleakly the second time his step faltered. Whether he went or stayed it couldn't make matters worse.

She wanted him out of her life and it to be back to how it had been before he'd appeared on the scene. Who could blame her? The farmer's boy had been brought into the conversation again. Maybe she was trying to tell him something and he'd been saved from making a fool of himself...again.

Tomorrow he would start making plans for his departure. Once his flight was booked and he'd given them an actual date of leaving at the surgery, he would feel less as if he were in some sort of stressed-out limbo.

The rest of his time at the lakeside practice would be an endurance test, but he would have to grin and bear it, while keeping in mind the thought that if Alexa had any sense she would marry Robbie Durkin.

That one wouldn't have any hang-ups with the past, or commitments to the future, though the thought of her sweet nakedness in the arms of Durkin made his stomach churn. She would be safe with him, though, in their quiet rural backwater.

He smiled grimly at the thought. The last thing Alexa was bothered about was being safe.

As Carol bloomed in her pregnancy, Alexa was pale and listless, and when her sister asked anxiously what ailed her, she said with painful flippancy, 'It's my love life that's gone all wrong, but I'll survive. Reece is going back soon and that will be that.'

The last thing she wanted was to put a blight on Carol's happiness and if she knew just how deep her despair was, her sister would be consumed with protective anxiety.

'So you've accepted that you haven't got a future to-gether?'

'I've had no choice, have I? But as I've just said, I'll cope. There are plenty of other fish in the sea.'

'Such as Robbie Durkin?'

Alexa had shrugged drooping shoulders.

'Maybe.'

She hadn't told Carol that she and Reece had made love. The hurt was still there, raw and angry, like a wound de-termined not to heal, and she couldn't bear to bring her pain out into the open.

Added to that she felt that her sister might think she'd

cheapened herself by letting it happen, and in a way she supposed she had.

Then came the news at the surgery. Dr Rowlinson was leaving at the end of the second week in December.

'So what do you think about that?' Beryl asked when they heard.

'Not a lot,' Alexa said bleakly. 'We've known from the start that he was only filling in after John's departure so it isn't exactly a surprise, is it?'

'And you're not upset?'

'No,' she lied. 'Why should I be?'

'No romance in the offing, then?'

Alexa shook her head as an alternative to further tampering with the truth. She hated lying, but neither could she tell anyone about the despair that was weighing her down.

The cause of it was keeping a low profile. Ever since his disastrous handling of the situation he'd created that night at the garden flat he'd been treading warily so as not to hurt her further.

When the notice about his departure had gone up on the board in Reception he had gone out of his way to avoid the nurse's room. Then a teenage lad with an abscess on his arm had presented himself and he'd had to take him there to have it dressed.

After Reece had drained it he told her in clipped tones, 'I'll leave him to you now, Alexa. A sterile dressing and another appointment in a couple of days, I think.'

She was pale. There were dark smudges beneath her eyes and it took all his control not to fold her in his arms and tell her to hell with the rest of the world, this was where he wanted to be. But he'd been going to do that, hadn't he? Until she'd told him that she couldn't wait for him to go.

He wasn't to know that she'd sensed his concern and that the last thing she wanted was his pity. As she dealt with the young man's arm she was seized with a sudden urge to take the wind out of his sails. Turning to him, she dredged up a smile and said, 'I see you've fixed a date for leaving the practice.'

'Yes, that's correct,' he said slowly.

'We'll have to see about giving you a big send-off, then.'

His expression held ironic disbelief.

'You mean with a rocket in a strategic place to commemorate the havoc I've wrought?'

She ignored that and went on to say, 'How about a party here after hours? I know everyone would be in favour of the idea, including John and Liz.'

'I didn't think you'd want anything like that.'

'Which just goes to show how little you know me. I'm always ready for a party,' she told him with brittle lightness.

'If that's the case you'll be pleased to know that someone else is planning one for this weekend at my place, mainly for practice staff and friends.'

'Really? Who?'

'Rebecca.'

'What's the occasion?'

'To announce that her broken engagement is back on course and that a wedding is in the offing.'

Alexa goggled at him. The 'ice queen' had kept that quiet.

'So she gave up on you?'

'Rebecca was never interested in me,' he said in mild reproof. 'Her cold aloofness was a front to cover an aching heart, and the measure of it is that in me she found someone to talk to.'

'I see,' she said woodenly.

Not long ago she would have been delighted to know that Rebecca had no designs on Reece. But now it didn't matter either way, and if what he was saying was correct,

he other woman's way of hiding her heartache had been
much more dignified than her own, babbling on about a
farewell party for him that would be torture from the word
go.

But Annette, who was assisting her that morning, had
overheard her suggestion and before Alexa knew it the idea
had gone round the staff and been approved of wholeheart-
edly, so there would be no chance of backing out now.

Alexa stopped looking at the calendar over recent weeks.
It was too painful to see how the days were sliding away,
but suddenly another reason presented itself for checking
dates.

She opened her eyes one morning to the fact that something that should have happened a week ago hadn't. Her
first thought was that although her monthly cycle was rarely
irregular, maybe on this occasion the stress she was under
might have affected it.

But she was a nurse, for heaven's sake, she told herself
dismally. The reason was far more likely to be from natural
causes, such as being pregnant.

She turned her face into the pillow as her heart raced
inside her. It was possible. On the mad wave of desire that
she and Reece had been riding on that never-to-be-forgotten
night, the thought of an unwanted pregnancy had been the
last thing in her mind.

Yet a child that was theirs would never be unwanted. At
least, not as far as she was concerned. If she couldn't have
the father, at least she would have his child.

The clock beside her bed was ticking away. Another day
at the practice was calling and, telling herself that it was
too soon to be thinking she might be pregnant, she eased
herself off the bed and padded across to the shower.

But every time she saw Reece her insides clenched. He

would have a right to be told if she was carrying his child
and what would happen if she was?

Knowing him, he wouldn't leave her to face it alone, and
then she would be burdened with guilt in case he felt that
she'd ensnared him into a bondage of responsibility.

By the end of the week she was vomiting in the mornings
and was grateful that Carol wasn't around to see her, as
one pregnant woman would be quick to spot another.

After a visit to a chemist out of the area the answer she'd
been expecting was there. She was pregnant with Reece's
child.

During the rest of the day her mind was in a chaos. Only
one thought was clear. She wasn't going to tell Reece. If
he ever wanted to be with her permanently it would have
to be of his own free will...not just because he was going
to be a father.

Rebecca's re-engagement party was the night after Alexa
had confirmed that she was carrying Reece's child, and she
had never felt less like attending a social occasion.

For one thing, it was being held at the house that he was
renting from the Durkins, which was virtually on Robbie's
doorstep, and if there was one person she didn't want to
see in light of recent events it was the farmer's son.

Her relationship with him had been friendly enough and
essentially platonic, which hadn't been his choice, but
Alexa had sensed that he was biding his time.

As she dressed for the party she thought pensively that
if Robbie had known who he was competing with, he
would have called it a day long ago.

Taking a smart black dress from the wardrobe, she observed it with critical eyes. How did she want to look?
Elegantly subdued? It would certainly be in keeping with
the way she was feeling.

Or, holding a beige linen trouser suit against her body, did she want to look smart but not dowdy?

In the end she chose to wear a filmy dress of tangerine silk that turned her hair to flame and her skin to smooth cream. It was a gesture. No way did she want Reece to see her looking anything less than beautiful, whether he wanted her or not.

When he answered the door and saw her standing there his eyes darkened, but his voice was even enough as he bade her enter. The staff from the practice were all there dressed up to the nines, with John and Liz looking on benignly.

As she looked around her Alexa thought that it had been a very strange week, and tonight she was seeing the climax of it in the change that happiness had wrought in Rebecca.

As the blonde doctor introduced her to the pleasant middle-aged lecturer who was responsible for the radiant woman by his side, Alexa's spirits sank even lower.

What had she done to deserve the kind of deal that the fates were serving up to her? she thought dismally as she caught Reece's eyes upon her from across the room. She was carrying his precious seed inside her and he didn't know. Nor was she likely to.

Suddenly he was beside her.

'You look pale,' he said briefly. 'Are you all right?'

She managed a smile.

'Yes, of course. I've only just arrived. I've not had time to get into the swing of things.'

Who was she kidding? Certainly not herself. She'd never felt less like partying in her life.

But as the evening progressed she livened up. It's a celebration, not a funeral wake, she told herself, and if you don't perk up Reece is going to guess there's something wrong.

So she danced a bit, gossiped a bit, and before she knew it farewells were being said.

'I'll see you home, Alexa,' Reece offered.

She shook her head. 'I think not. It's only five minutes' walk and you might want me to invite you in for a coffee.'

He sighed.

'All right. Message received. But I shall ring you shortly to make sure you're safely home.'

It was close on midnight and just as she reached the gate of Craith House the very person she didn't want to see appeared with two of his friends.

All three were in high spirits after a night in the town and Robbie said boisterously, 'The Soames woman told me that you were all going to a shindig at the farm cottage. How did it go?'

'It was fine,' she said with more enthusiasm than it warranted, and when they showed no signs of moving on she stayed chatting with them at the gate, aware that by now Reece would be on the phone, checking to see if she was home.

She was being childish and was aware of it, but she wanted him to realise that he wasn't in her life any more. That he couldn't move in and out of it at will.

As she put her key in the lock she could hear the instrument's strident ring, but by the time she was inside it had stopped and she knew that unless she rang back immediately he would be there within minutes to see what was going on.

'I'm back,' she said when he answered.

'What took you so long?' he snapped. 'I was about to come round.'

'No need,' she told him smoothly. 'I've been chatting to Robbie and his friends at the gate.'

'And that was more important than putting my mind at rest?'

'Depends how you look at it.'

'Oh, I see. You've finally decided that I don't matter. In that case I'll say goodnight, Alexa. Sleep well.'

When he'd hung up she stood looking down at the receiver. 'Sleep well,' he'd said. How well would Reece sleep if he knew that he'd given her a child?

As Carol's pregnancy advanced she had no idea that her sister was in a similar condition. Alexa was unhappy at not being able to confide in her but, aware of the loving bond between them, she felt that if Carol knew she would insist on Reece being told that he had made her pregnant.

She intended to tell her sister about the baby as soon as he'd gone, but until then it had to be her secret. There was no way she wanted him to change his plans because of what had happened.

Her conversation with John all those weeks ago kept going through her mind. The elderly GP had had no doubts about how much the job meant to Reece, and she wasn't going to be the one responsible for taking him away from it.

It was a strange feeling on the days when there were antenatal clinics at the surgery. Soon she would attending as one of the mothers-to-be, but at such an early stage of her pregnancy she could afford to wait a little while before joining them.

On a grey November day, Alexa was dismayed to find that Rebecca was taking the afternoon off and Reece had stepped in to take the clinic in her place.

The thought of working with him in such an atmosphere was painful to say the least. Amongst all the women present there would be one pregnancy that he didn't know about, and she was wondering how she would cope.

You've got to, she told herself. Reece misses nothing. One bleep out of you and he'll be on your case.

They'd spoken only rarely since the night of Rebecca's party. She knew that he'd been angry at the way she'd spurned his concern, but it was just too bad. If it kept him at a distance, so be it.

As long as he didn't touch her, or seek her out when she was alone, she was in control, and after the way she'd gushed about Robbie, she doubted whether he'd do anything like that. But there was always the feeling that Reece was watching her. That he was tuned in to what was going on in her life.

Although he couldn't be. He hadn't caught on to the fact that she was pregnant, and at the thought of what might happen if he ever did, she fought off a nausea attack that had nothing to do with her condition.

Reece was aware that taking the antenatal clinic would throw them together, but he hadn't had much choice. Rebecca and her fiancé were making an offer on a house and had an appointment with their solicitor. Bryan was taking the diabetic clinic, so it left only him to deal with the mums-to-be.

Everything was ready when he went into the nurse's room. Alexa had laid out the antenatal equipment. And now she was waiting, seemingly cool and composed, for the clinic to start.

He felt his nerve ends slacken. She was going to be all right. He hadn't broken her heart or anything so dramatic. She was young and resilient. Alexa would bounce back.

Yet she was thinner. The smooth lines of her face seemed to have hollowed, but as usual her efficiency was in full force.

'So, have I passed the test?' she asked coolly.

'What do you mean?'

'You're looking me over as if I'm under the microscope.'

Reece laughed.

'Yes, of course you've passed the test. You always do.'

'I'm not sure that I want to know what you mean by that,' she told him.

He didn't take her up on it. Instead he asked, 'Have you lost weight?'

'I don't know. I might have.'

'The scales are there.'

'Yes, so I see.'

If she'd lost weight the reason wasn't far to seek. She was still suffering from pregnancy sickness. Soon it would be the other way and she'd be putting weight on. But by that time Reece would be somewhere at the other side of the world.

The patients were arriving and she wasn't sorry. It saved any further talk between them. As they worked side by side for the rest of the afternoon Alexa pushed away her own cares for a while.

Beryl was on duty as practice nurse during the evening surgery so Alexa was free to go once the clinic was over, and she wasted no time in doing so.

But Reece caught her up on the car park.

'What's the hurry?' he wanted to know.

'I've got a hair appointment.'

To her surprise he opened the car door and slid into the seat beside her. Running his hand over his own dark head, he said, 'I could do with a cut. I'll come along if you don't mind. I imagine they'll be able to fit me in at this hour without an appointment.'

She almost groaned out loud. Couldn't he see that she wanted to distance herself from him?

Her hair was long and thick and on a sudden impulse she'd decided to have it cut really short. A new look for a new beginning, she'd told herself unconvincingly, although she was being a bit premature. Reece was still in her orbit and likely to be so until the plane that was taking him away from her took off.

Seated at the opposite side of the salon, he was watching her in the mirror, and his jaw went slack when he saw the long swathes of her hair falling to the floor.

What was Alexa thinking of? he thought numbly. Letting the girl hack her hair off like that! His own cut was finished and he was on his feet and crossing to where she was before he'd had time to think.

'Are you crazy?' he asked quietly, and, bending, he picked up a lock of her hair.

Looking down on the bright, burnished strands lying on his open palm, he exclaimed, 'Why have it chopped off? Your hair was beautiful.'

She swung round in the chair and his face went slack for a second time.

What was left of her hair was now in a short, curly cut that accentuated the fine-boned contours of her face and made her beautiful hazel eyes seem even more luminous.

'New haircut—new beginning,' she informed him breezily in a repeat of what she'd said to herself earlier. But it was as if he wasn't listening.

'You look enchanting,' he said gravely, 'but, then, I should have known you would.' And with that he went to the counter, paid his bill and went.

Unlike Alexa, Reece hadn't finished for the day. He was taking evening surgery, and by the time it was over and he'd had his evening meal, it was getting late.

'What do you think of our shorn lamb?' Carol asked laughingly as he was on the point of leaving Craith House.

He smiled. She wasn't to know that part of the shearing lay curled between the pages of his diary.

'Stunning,' he said lightly, and then, with his voice deepening added, 'Look after her, Carol.'

'Shouldn't *you* be doing that?' she said, suddenly serious. 'That's what Alexa wants.'

He sighed.

'Yes. I know. But I'm afraid we met at the wrong time and what we want isn't always the best thing for us.'

It was Carol's turn to sigh now.

'If you say so, I suppose.' Then, as if accepting that there was no more to be said on that subject, she went on, 'You'll be leaving around the time that my baby is born, won't you?'

He nodded.

'Yes. I will, and in the meantime it's business as usual. They're giving me a send-off party at the practice. It was Alexa's idea, but I have a feeling that she's having second thoughts.'

'I can imagine. She'll hate to see you go.'

'So why not let me depart without any fuss?'

'Because Alexa has a lot of pride…and the courage to cope with being left behind.'

He had his hand on the doorhandle and with a twisted smile he told her, 'Don't say any more, Carol. It may not seem like it, but we both have her best interests at heart.' And with that he went. A sombre figure, disappearing into the dark night.

'Was that Reece you were talking to?' Alexa asked some seconds later. 'I thought I heard his voice.'

Carol eyed her carefully, having no wish to add to her sister's misery with regard to Reece Rowlinson.

'Yes. I was asking him what he thought about your new haircut.'

'And what did he say?'

'That it was stunning.'

'"Stunned" was how he looked when he came charging to my side in the hairdresser's, demanding to know what I was doing.'

'Reece would think you looked marvellous whatever you did,' Carol said. 'Can't you persuade him to stay?'

'No!' Alexa told her flatly. 'He has to stay because he wants to. Not because he's been persuaded.'

'OK. I get the message. And, Alexa, on the same subject, what's this about a farewell party for Reece? Don't you think it's rather turning the knife?'

She shrugged wearily.

'It was only a suggestion, but Annette heard it and before I'd got my breath back it was all round the surgery, and you know what the staff there are like. Anything for a get-together. From just a drink after hours on the practice premises, it's now grown to a night at the theatre and a meal afterwards.'

During which I shall probably give the game away by vomiting, she thought as Carol observed her anxiously.

'And are you sure you can cope with all that, feeling the way you do about him?' she asked.

'I can cope,' Alexa said with bleak confidence.

And she would, until the second his plane took off, and then it would be time to face up to the future. Time to confide to Carol that she, too, was pregnant and to take the necessary steps towards bringing Reece's child into the world.

If she was being unfair to him by keeping her pregnancy secret, she couldn't help it. She'd fallen in love with him at their very first meeting and nothing was going to change that. But if she told him about it, she knew he would stay for the baby's sake and the last thing she wanted from him was an act of honourable duty.

The fact that he was stubbornly refusing to involve her in the kind of life he was committed to was understandable, but it didn't make it any less hurtful. He'd never said that he loved her, so maybe he didn't. Perhaps to him she was just a passing fancy, which made it all the more imperative that she keep her condition to herself.

CHAPTER NINE

IT WAS a time of year when the surgery was especially busy. As the weather became colder, coughs, colds and all that went with them were keeping the GPs and the practice nurses fully occupied.

And added to that, as far as the nurses were concerned, there was a constant queue of the elderly and those likely to suffer chest complaints, waiting to be given the flu and pneumonia vaccines.

Alexa was relieved to be so busy. It gave her less time to think about what was happening in her life. She'd accepted that Reece was going and knew that the misery she was facing now would be nothing to how she would feel when he'd left.

It was still hard to believe that she was pregnant by him, and if it hadn't been for the fact that she rose each morning feeling totally nauseous she might have thought she'd dreamt it.

Fortunately, by the time she presented herself at the surgery the sickness had passed, otherwise it might have caused some awkward questions.

Carol's baby was due soon and in the excitement of the fast-approaching birth Alexa was putting on a show of high spirits that disappeared like water down a drain the moment she was alone in her own place.

As she drove home one night after a particularly tiring day the feeling of guilt was upon her because Carol still didn't know about the changes that were taking place in her life.

Yet she supposed that if she felt guilty about anyone's

ignorance it should be Reece's. But *he* wasn't the only one who could dig his heels in. If he could be unrelenting, so could she.

In any case, if he ever did come back to the Lakes he would find out for himself that she'd had his child. She could imagine it, them coming face to face. She holding the hand of a tiny girl with wide hazel eyes and chestnut hair in pigtails. Or with a sturdy dark-haired boy galloping along beside her, and Reece transfixed at the sight.

But her mind was leaping ahead. Those sorts of day-dreams would get her exactly nowhere.

There were more pressing matters to be dealt with, such as facing up to the role of a single parent and bringing their child safely into the world. They were the priorities in her life. The distant future would have to look after itself.

The sad thing about it all was that the situation she found herself in was usually due to the break-up of a relationship or an illicit affair. Theirs was neither of those things.

She wasn't fighting another woman's claims on him. It was the memory of Natalie's deceit that he hadn't forgotten, along with the welfare of needy souls in different corners of the world.

Long ago he'd asked a woman to share his life and she hadn't been willing to accept the lows along with the highs of marrying him.

It must have shaken his confidence badly as he wasn't going to risk that kind of rejection again. But he'd never given *her* the chance to tell him that as far as she was concerned she would follow him to the ends of the earth.

The opportunity hadn't been on offer and now, unwittingly, he'd provided another reason why she should stay behind.

'We're out of the flu vaccine,' he'd told her that morning, 'so if anyone comes in asking for it, tell them that fresh supplies are due any time.'

He was observing her with his dark watchful gaze again. 'I presume that you've had yours?'

Alexa hesitated. If she were to say yes it would be a lie, and 'no' would have him immediately wanting to know why.

The fact of the matter was that in her present state she wasn't prepared to have any injections until her pregnancy was established and being monitored.

The flu jab had been known to give its recipient a mild attack of the very thing it was there to prevent, and in her case she could do without that sort of complication at present.

'Er...yes,' she told him evasively, and prayed that he wouldn't pursue it.

He didn't. Bryan was hovering to say that there would be a practice meeting later in the morning with regard to Reece's replacement, and as it was a subject that they both wanted to avoid, he went.

Reece didn't come to the meeting. There was no point as it didn't concern him and it left him free to hold the fort while the others were thus engaged.

The senior partner informed them that there were two prospective candidates for the post—a middle-aged GP who was moving into Cumbria from the south for family reasons and a woman doctor who had been hospital-based and was ready for a change.

Alexa found her mind wandering as the appointment was discussed. For one thing, it would still be Bryan and Rebecca who made the decision. The rest of them would have no say in the matter. It was merely for their information that the meeting had been called.

But the main reason for her lack of interest was that it only went to emphasise the fact that Reece was going, and she only tuned in when in conclusion Bryan mentioned the send-off party for the man in question.

'Just to remind you all,' he said, 'Reece's last day with us will soon be here, and we are bidding him farewell with a visit to the theatre and a meal afterwards. Will those who intend going to the performance of *Les Misérables*, please, let us know so that we can arrange a block booking?'

Alexa stifled a groan. Her suggestion of a send-off for Reece had been made to him in a moment of bravado and she would have retracted it at the first opportunity if it hadn't been overheard by Annette and been taken up by the rest of the staff.

Since then the idea had snowballed from a drink at the wine bar to a show and a meal afterwards. It was ironic that they'd chosen *Les Misérables*. It would fit in with her mood exactly.

As they all filed out Beryl said, 'Who's collecting for a farewell present?'

'I've no idea,' Alexa told her flatly, 'but it certainly isn't going to be me.'

That really would have been turning the knife.

'So, is my replacement sorted?' Reece asked some minutes later when they came face to face outside the nurse's room.

'I've no idea,' Alexa told him stonily. 'Why? Are you interested?'

'Don't do this to me, Alexa,' he said sombrely. 'You'll thank me for it one day.'

'It will be a long while coming,' she told him in the same cold tone.

Most of the time she was in control, but during the practice meeting the inevitability of it all had hit her like a sledgehammer and now Reece was calmly asking if they'd found someone to fill the gap that he'd been bridging.

There would be no problem finding another GP. It was the empty place that he would be leaving in her heart that was making her want to hit out at him. In moments like these the hurt came bursting through and no power on earth could have kept it back.

'Fair enough,' he said tonelessly, and went back to his patients.

He'd been going to ask what the arrangements were for the farewell that they were planning for him but, having already put his foot in it, he'd decided that it wasn't the moment.

A big fuss was the last thing he wanted, and when Alexa had suggested it he'd been dumbstruck. He would have thought that the sooner he was on his way the better as far as she was concerned, but she'd insisted that she was up for a party. So maybe his departure wasn't going to hit her as hard as he'd thought.

But the fact remained that of late she lacked the zest that had so attracted him to her at their first meeting, and the blame lay at his door.

It was ironic to think that he was leaving Rebecca a much happier woman than when he'd first met her, and Alexa, who had stood out amongst them all like a bright star, had lost her sparkle.

But, then, so had he. Not so much his sparkle, but his single-mindedness of purpose, and it was only grim determination that was keeping him going.

'I'm flying to Australia to visit relatives over Christmas,' his next patient said with a distinct lack of enthusiasm, 'and I'm worried about blood clots in my legs. They've been on about it in the media, how long flights with restricted movement can cause that sort of thing, and it's made me nervous.'

He was a lean, fit-looking seventy-year-old with a record of very little illness, but there was no doubt that the man was extremely worried about the forthcoming flight.

'We all get thickening of the arteries as we grow older,'

Reece told him, 'but I don't see any reference to that sort of problem in your notes, Mr Norris. My advice to you is what you will already have heard on television. Take aspirin before flying and move about the aircraft occasionally.

'I know it will be a long flight, which does increase the risk of blood clots, but I'm going to examine you and if I find no cause for alarm then I think you can go with an easy mind, as long as you do what I've suggested. Would you unbutton your shirt, please?'

When he'd finished Reece smiled into the man's worried eyes. 'You're a pretty fit specimen for your age, Mr Norris. Heart seems OK. Your blood pressure is normal. There are a few enlarged veins on your legs, but they don't appear to be in a critical state.

'Go ahead, enjoy your holiday. The aspirin will help to prevent coagulation, and avoiding sitting in one position for too long will also be beneficial.'

'So you think I should go, then, Doctor?'

Reece nodded.

'Why not? That sort of an opportunity doesn't always come twice.'

When the elderly man had gone Reece thought that Mr Norris wasn't the only one about to embark on a long flight and he'd have liked to have bet that the old guy would be a lot happier than he himself when he reached his destination.

His mind went back again to his forthcoming departure. The sooner it was over the better. It had been like a long-drawn-out agony ever since he'd booked his flight. Seeing Alexa, aching to hold her, and yet knowing that he daren't allow himself to weaken.

The fact that Carol's and Tom's baby would be arriving soon after he'd gone was fortuitous. Alexa would be absorbed with her new niece or nephew, which would occupy her mind to some extent.

While, on his part, what would he have to take the pain away? The memory of their one and only act of love?

He was gripped with a sudden need to talk to her. To know what was in her mind. It was all right telling himself that the sooner he went the better, but that was the coward's way out. He couldn't turn back now, but at least he could make sure that Alexa understood that his going wasn't because he didn't love her.

At the first opportunity he would take her to one side, and it couldn't come quickly enough.

The man who was going to Australia was followed by a haggard-looking woman in her forties who wanted to give up smoking.

She'd started in her teens and was now on forty cigarettes a day. Patches, chewing gum and an imitation cigarette to hold had all been non-productive, and now she had come to the surgery for help.

'I'm going to put you in touch with the smoking cessation co-ordinator in the area,' he told her. 'There's a therapy centre that you will be invited to attend that will help you far more than anything you've tried before. But you need to remember that to stop smoking you have to want to do it with every fibre of your being, otherwise it won't work.'

She nodded glumly and when Reece told her he'd like to sound her chest she said, 'It's not good, Doctor. I've had bronchitis twice this year.'

When he'd finished his face was sombre. 'You're right, it isn't. You've got a chest infection now. It's not serious, but it will be if I don't give you something for it…and if nothing else works, the state of your health should give you the purpose that you need.'

As he handed her the necessary information about the non-smoking clinic Reece felt that perhaps he hadn't been very sympathetic, but she did need to stop the habit, and a softly, softly, approach wasn't going to fire her determination.

It was an unhealthy habit, but he would never make light of the difficulty of overcoming it. He'd seen countless people give it up, sometimes for long periods, and then become addicted again in times of stress or even for no particular reason.

Robbie Durkin called round at the garden flat that evening and when Alexa let him in he said immediately, 'Why are you avoiding me, Lexy? Is it because you think I'm unhealthy?'

The last thing she felt like was a heart-to-heart with Robbie, but he did look less than his usual cocksure self and she did know that today he'd had the results from some tests that Reece had instigated.

'Unhealthy!' she cried. 'You look all right to me. Is it the test results that you're on about?'

'Yeah. I've got a cyst.'

'But it isn't cancerous, is it?'

'No, it's benign. Whatever that means.'

She had to laugh.

'It means that it's not malignant, so you've no need to worry. They'll probably get rid of it with laser treatment or medication. Lots of folk have that kind of thing but in most cases they're harmless.'

He shrugged his shoulders.

'Yeah, but my bladder of all things! I'm not going to tell my mates.'

Alexa found herself laughing again.

'Why not? We all have one.'

He was moving towards her with his confidence restored.

'Yeah, I suppose so,' he said. 'Like we have mouths, lips and...'

His eyes were on the soft mounds of her breasts inside the cotton top she was wearing.

She put out a hand to ward him off and he stopped and glared at her.

'So you *have* gone off me?' he growled.

'Look, Robbie,' she said, finding patience from somewhere, 'as far as I'm concerned, we're just friends, and I've never led you to think otherwise. I'm in love with someone else, if you must know.'

'Not Rowlinson, surely? I can tell he has the hots for you, but I haven't seen you together much.'

He wasn't wrong there, she thought grimly. It was a low-key love affair in every sense of the word. If 'love affair' was the correct description.

'Who I care for is my own business,' she said as he prepared to make a sulky exit.

But knowing only too well the humiliation of rejection, when he opened the door to go she gave him a hug and a fleeting kiss on the cheek which he immediately seized upon by quickly turning his head so that it landed on his lips.

Then, grabbing her to him, he kissed her back, until with her fists on his chest she pushed him away and closed the door on him with an angry thud.

So much for sympathy, she thought dismally as she threw herself down onto the sofa. That one just couldn't take no for an answer.

Outside, Reece had just put one foot on the path in front of Alexa's flat when the door was flung open and Durkin appeared, with Alexa close behind.

He stepped into the shadows and watched their passionate embrace, granite-faced, before turning to go back to his car.

Yet wasn't his darling girl doing what he'd told her to

do? Finding someone else to love her? If the muscle-bound young farmer knew what love was.

When he got back to the house he flung the rest of his stuff into the cases that were waiting and locked them with grim decisiveness. He'd been right all along. A clean break was what was required. No point in prolonging the agony. And after what he'd just seen it looked as if Alexa was thinking along the same lines.

Carol and Tom had declined the offer to know the sex of their child and Alexa wondered if she would feel inclined to do the same when the time came.

She was keeping an eye on her blood pressure, taking vitamin supplements to make up for the early morning vomiting and resting in the evenings to make up for the stressful days at the surgery. In other words, generally taking a sensible approach to her pregnancy from a health point of view.

Mentally it was a different matter. The thought was constantly intruding that this should be one of the happiest times of her life and it wasn't, far from it in fact.

She wasn't daunted at the thought of bringing up a child alone. Cope she would, but when she thought of how different it could be, her determination crumbled.

Looking back to that day on the lake when she'd first met Reece, she wished it had never happened.

But it would have made no difference if it hadn't. He'd already been a guest at Craith House and due to become part of the practice any day, so it was almost as if it had been pre-ordained.

And was what had happened since meant to be? she asked herself after she'd calmed down after Robbie's visit. There must be dozens of men with uncomplicated lives that she could have fallen in love with, but she had to find the one who wouldn't budge an inch.

The clock was ticking on. An early night wouldn't do her any harm, and tomorrow she would awaken, as on every other day, to the realisation that soon would come the dreaded farewell.

She was aroused in the winter dawn by Tom, who told her worriedly, 'Carol is getting pains. They're quite bad, but not at regular intervals.'

'Are there any other symptoms to indicate that she's in labour?' Alexa asked as they hurried back to the guest house.

'Not as yet. Only the pains.'

Carol had her coat on and her bag beside her when they went inside, and Alexa ran across and hugged her.

'You're a week early, Caro,' she said, 'but that's not unusual. Do you think this is it?'

'I don't know,' she said uneasily. 'I'm getting pains every now and again, but nothing else has happened yet. However, I'm not taking any chances. Tom is going to take me to hospital.'

'Yes, of course,' Alexa agreed. 'Lie down on the couch for a moment. If you get any pains while I'm feeling your stomach, tell me. I'm no midwife, but I do assist in the antenatal clinic at the surgery and have seen a few pregnant mums in my time.'

The baby was very low in the uterus, which was to be expected with the time of birth so near, but there was no dilatation and Alexa couldn't pick up on any contractions, even when the pain was there.

'What do you think?' Carol asked anxiously when they'd raised her to a sitting position.

'You could be in slow labour,' Alexa told her. 'On the other hand, the pain could be muscular or the baby has moved and is pressing on a nerve.'

'Come along, darling,' Tom said, helping her to her feet. 'Let's get you to hospital.'

When he'd tucked Carol into the car he said to Alexa, 'Will you see to the breakfasts if I'm not back by half seven?'

'Yes, of course,' she told him. 'I'll ring the surgery to say I'm taking a day off. Don't worry about a thing. Just take care of Carol.'

It was mad during the breakfast hour even though Alexa knew the routine, but luckily the guest house wasn't full. It was just that those booked in were big eaters and the young girl who was waiting on tables had only started the week before.

She hadn't rang the surgery yet as it wouldn't be open but as the clock began to slide down to eight-thirty it would soon have to be done.

'What's going on here?' Reece's voice said suddenly from the open doorway. 'Old Durkin said he saw Tom driving out of the village looking very fraught when he was going to the sheds to do the milking.

'He could see that he had one of you with him, but wasn't sure which as he was going quite fast. Obviously it wasn't you, so it had to be Carol. Is she in labour?'

Alexa had turned from the stove with a face as red as the tomatoes that she was frying and was observing him in some surprise. Reece was the last person she'd expected to see at this hour.

'We're not sure,' she told him briefly. 'She was in pain, but I'm not sure if they were labour pains.'

'I see,' he said, and she heard relief in his voice. 'Logic said that Tom's urgency must be something to do with Carol, but I had to come round to make sure that you were all right.'

She laughed but there was no mirth in it.

'Well, as you can see, I am. The only thing I'm suffering from is the trauma of feeding their guests until Tom gets back…and in any case, would it have mattered if something had been wrong with me?'

'Of course it would! You know damn well it would.'

'Do I?' she asked as the tomatoes started to burn. 'And suppose something happens to me when you've gone. You won't be able to fuss over me then, will you? Because you won't know anything about it. My welfare will be the last thing on your mind.'

'And is something likely to happen to you in my absence?' he asked, ignoring the comment about her welfare.

Keen, dark eyes were watching her face, and she knew if she wasn't careful he would start asking more questions. If she didn't fob him off quickly enough, he might just tune in to her condition.

'No, of course not,' she said with quick flippancy. 'I was just generalising.'

Reece was taking off his jacket, and as if the previous exchange of words had never been he said, 'What can I do to help?'

'Nothing. We're back,' Tom's voice said from behind them, and as Alexa turned from the spattering frying-pan she saw her sister and brother-in-law in the doorway.

Carol threw her a wry smile.

'It was a false alarm, Alexa,' she said. 'The baby was pressing on a nerve like you said. So you're off the hook for the time being.'

To Reece she said gratefully, 'It's good of you to offer to help, but I think there are folks down at the surgery who need you both more than us.

'We were caught on the hop with the pains coming during the night. But if they'd kept me in Tom would have immediately called on the temporary staff that we've hired to cover the event and the weeks after it. Alexa only got roped in to see to the breakfasts.' She turned to her sister. 'You are a treasure. I don't know what I'd do without you.'

That did it. The affection in her sister's voice brought tears to Alexa's eyes. Theirs was a loving bond that would always be there. If only the same deep well of tenderness was on offer from the man who had rushed round to Craith House consumed with anxiety that she might be hurt or ill, and yet was prepared to walk out of her life without a backward glance.

'I'm going to get changed,' she choked, and with head bent pushed her way past him.

'So no new arrival yet?' Beryl said when she arrived at the surgery.

Alexa shook her head.

'No. It was a false alarm. Carol and Tom were back within a couple of hours.'

Her friend smiled.

'Knowing the unborn infant fraternity, it will probably come when you are all least prepared.'

Reece came into the nurse's room at that moment and with a quick glance at Alexa asked, 'Have you cooled down?'

As Beryl observed them curiously she said stiffly, 'Yes, thanks.'

'And did you have time for any breakfast yourself?'

'Er...no, but I'm not very hungry.'

It had been a miracle that for once she hadn't felt nauseous. That would have been all she needed! But he did have a point. She shouldn't be missing her food under the circumstances and when he suggested that she leave what she was doing and go and have something to eat, for once she didn't argue. Even though she felt like telling him to stop fussing. That it was too late for concern.

'And so what was all that about?' Beryl asked when she came back after a cup of tea and a bacon sandwich.

'Reece called in at Craith House this morning to see what was going on and he found me sweating over a hot stove, cooking breakfast for the guests. Even at this time of the year there's always someone staying there.'

Beryl was smiling.

'And he was worried that his favourite nurse wasn't getting her nourishment?'

'I doubt it,' Alexa said lightly. 'Unless he was concerned that any malnutrition on my part might create a staff shortage.'

'He's the one who's causing a staff shortage,' Beryl countered. 'He's one of the best doctors we've ever had, probably because he's way out of our league, but I do wish he'd stay.' With a twinkle in her eye she added, 'As much for your sake as anything.'

'Yes, well, don't hold your breath about that,' she said flatly. 'He'll be on that plane when it takes off. I guarantee it.'

As Reece prepared to face the sick and suffering of the day, he admitted to himself that he envied Alexa and her sister their close family bond.

He'd been without family himself for as long as he could remember, and even John's great kindness to him hadn't made up for the lack of kin.

Perhaps one day he would have a family of his own, but he was going the wrong way about it. If Natalie had been the right person he might have had growing children by now, he thought soberly, but then he would never have met Alexa.

Last night he'd succumbed again to the ache inside him, but he'd been prevented from making a fool of himself at this late date by the sight of her in Robbie Durkin's arms, and had had to admit that it would be the best thing all round if that relationship were to prosper.

When he'd seen her this morning, presiding over the breakfasts at Craith House, he'd been weak with relief to find her safe and well. But as she'd pointed out, her welfare wasn't his concern, either now or in the future. Soon he would be out of her life and sensibly she'd turned to someone else for comfort.

It wasn't surprising that he'd been thinking back to that time with Natalie. She was on the morning's list of patients and when she came flouncing in with her usual brash manner in evidence, he couldn't help comparing it with Alexa's open pleasantness.

Alexa was, or had been until he'd appeared on the scene, bright, bouncy and loving. With the children in their care she was gentle and reassuring, and to the adults she extended a service that was caring and efficient.

He doubted if Natalie had ever done a service for anyone in her life, but he was about to do one for her, and maybe for once she would be humble instead of arrogant.

Reception had phoned to ask her to come in. This morning he'd heard from the oncologist at the hospital where she was being treated that the cancer was reducing and that there was an excellent chance of a cure.

To his surprise she burst into tears when he told her the good tidings.

'Thank God!' she breathed, and gave a contrite smile. 'Though I don't deserve it, do I, Reece.'

He went round to the other side of the desk and put his arm around her shoulders.

'Everyone deserves a chance to get better, Natalie,' he told her gravely, 'but not everyone is chosen. You're not out of the woods yet, but it's a very good report so take it to heart and be happy.'

'And us?' she asked.

'You know the answer to that, I'm afraid. I'm leaving the Lakes in the very near future.'

She smiled and he thought that for once Natalie was in a likeable mood.

'Then good luck wherever you go and in whatever you do,' she said, and with new zest in her stride she went.

Alexa saw her go and thought that Reece had certainly given his beautiful ex-fiancée something to smile about. But that it was nothing to do with her, so she put it out of her mind.

CHAPTER TEN

RESISTING the urge to wear black in keeping with the occasion, Alexa did the exact opposite for Reece's farewell from the practice.

A turquoise silk blouse, tight cream trousers and high-heeled matching sandals were her choice for the gloomy occasion and when she surveyed herself in the mirror before leaving her garden flat, she was content that the reflection looking back at her was giving nothing away of inner turmoil.

It was giving no hint of pregnancy either, but that wasn't going to last long. Soon it would be obvious to everyone that she was carrying a child. But once Reece had gone there would be no need to conceal the fact.

'Shall I call for you tomorrow?' he'd said as they were leaving the surgery on the Friday night. 'I'll be passing Craith House on my way to the theatre.'

'No, thanks,' she'd said briefly. 'I'll make my own way there.'

'Suit yourself,' had been his reply.

She was going to suit herself, she thought grimly. He didn't have to worry on that score. *He* was suiting *him*self!

And now, as the most miserable of *les misérables*, she was off to the event that she'd been dreading with a fixed smile on her lips and a dead weight in her heart.

What Reece's feelings were about the night ahead she didn't know and wasn't likely to find out. He would have to put on a show for all the staff who'd gone to so much trouble on his behalf.

She was the last to arrive in the foyer of the theatre and

she saw that it had been noted by him. A quick glance at the clock and his closed expression told their own story.

So what? she thought rebelliously. It was like going to the dentist. One didn't go early for that kind of appointment and neither did one for this.

As they filed into the seats that had been booked for them, Beryl was between Reece and herself and Alexa was thankful. But to her dismay, as they were on the point of seating themselves her friend took a swift backward step and manoeuvred Alexa into her place. There was nothing she could do without making a scene and so she settled herself meekly beside him.

Reece made no comment. He was reading the programme as if his life depended on it and Alexa wondered if he was giving her time to gather her wits.

It was a foregone conclusion that she would be totally aware of his nearness all through the performance. Their elbows were touching on the arm of the seat. She could smell his aftershave. See the fine dark hairs on the back of the hand that lay loosely on his knee.

Suddenly they were moments to savour instead of an endurance test, and it took all her strength of will not to reach out and touch him.

When they went into the foyer at the interval for refreshments Beryl asked mischievously, 'So, did I do right?'

'In what way?' Alexa asked innocently.

The other woman laughed.

'Putting you next to Reece.'

'It makes no odds either way,' she said dismissively. 'He's leaving tomorrow, no matter what. So what good could it do?'

'For one thing, it will give you the chance to tell him something that he ought to know.'

Alexa stopped in her tracks.

'And what is that supposed to mean?'

'That you're pregnant.'

The colour had left her face.

'You guessed?'

'I'm a nurse, aren't I?' Beryl said prosaically. 'For one thing you're feeling nauseous all the time, aren't you?'

'Not all the time. Just some of it. You won't tell Reece, will you, Beryl?' Alexa pleaded. 'He might feel he has to stay because I'm pregnant and I don't want him here for that reason.'

'Of course I won't tell him,' she said levelly, 'but *you* should.'

Alexa shook her head, but before she could say anything further Reece was bearing down on them with the drinks they'd ordered and Beryl, making another opportunity for them to talk, moved away to where the receptionists were grouped.

With glasses in hand, they stood in a small oasis of silence amongst the theatre crowd, neither of them wanting to be the first to speak. But at last, as if the words were being dragged out of him, Reece said, 'In view of the way you feel about me going, would it be too much to ask that we allow ourselves a few moments to say goodbye tomorrow morning? John is driving me to Preston where I'm catching a train to Manchester Airport, but I could be at our special place by the lake at nine o'clock.'

She was dumbstruck. What game was he playing? Whatever it was, it was a cruel one. But she hadn't the strength of will to refuse, grasping at straws though it might be. However, she wasn't going to give in so easily.

'I don't know. I'll have to think about it. Personally I think you have a cheek to ask it of me, but, then, you're a law unto yourself, aren't you, Reece?'

'I don't want a lecture,' he said stiffly. 'Just say yes or no.'

'I prefer to say maybe,' she told him as Rebecca and

Bryan loomed up in front of them, and he had to be satisfied with that.

Alexa didn't hear a word of the second half of the show because her mind was in chaos. Did she want to let herself in for more heartache? she kept asking herself as she observed his non-revealing profile. Yet she might never see him again.

Of course she was going to meet him. She was crazy to even think of not going. There was time for Reece to change his mind. But she still wouldn't try to make him stay.

The meal was a cheerful affair, with everyone drinking too much and sensibly bringing out their mobile phones to call for taxis. Only Alexa and Reece were keeping clear of the wine, and she knew that even if she hadn't been pregnant, she wouldn't have touched a drop anyway. If there was one thing she wanted to remember clearly for all time, it was Reece on this last night.

As the staff were all crowding round him outside the restaurant, saying their farewells and promising to keep in touch, she slipped away. She couldn't bear the thought of being surrounded by onlookers as she said her goodbyes, and in any case there was tomorrow to do that…by the lake.

At ten minutes to nine she was ready. Breakfast hadn't been a choice. She was too pent up to eat. Across at Craith House Carol was in the kitchen, clearing up after breakfast. Alexa could see her through the kitchen window and they waved to each other.

Suddenly her sister's expression changed and she saw her crouched over the sink as if in pain. The baby! Was that why Carol was holding her middle and gasping for breath?

Alexa was across there in a flash, and as she flung herself

into the kitchen Carol cried, 'It's coming, Alexa. The baby!'

'I'll phone for an ambulance,' she said swiftly. 'Where on earth is Tom?'

'Gone to the cash and carry,' Carol gasped, and as Alexa ran towards Reception to make the call, she cried, 'Hurry, Alexa! Please!'

When she came back Carol was still doubled up with pain, and running into the dining room Alexa grabbed one of the white tablecloths that were her sister's pride and joy.

Throwing it down on to the floor in front of her, she said urgently, 'Lie down, Carol, while I see what's going on.'

When her sister cried out again she told her, 'Take deep breaths, and whatever you do, don't push until I've examined you.'

As Carol eased herself down onto the floor she said, 'I've been having twinges ever since that false alarm, but they're not twinges now...it's agony.'

'It's going to be a fast birth from the looks of it,' Alexa told her. 'You're fully dilated. Keep taking deep breaths and don't push until I tell you.'

'I've got to! I can't stop myself!' Carol gasped.

'Just hang on for a few seconds and then you can push all you want.'

'I'll try, but it won't be for long,' she croaked.

'Right. Now you can push,' Alexa told her some seconds later, and within a short time she cried, 'I can see the baby's head. Keep pushing, Carol, darling.'

With one last shuddering thrust the baby was out and Alexa whooped, 'You have a daughter! A beautiful little girl! Here, take her, while I cope with what comes next.'

At that moment there was a screech of tyres outside on the drive and as Alexa was apprehensively observing the cord two paramedics came hurrying into the kitchen.

They were the most welcome sight she'd ever seen and

her nerve ends slackened when one of them said, 'If you'd like to get some warm water and find us a soft towel, we'll take over.'

She was a woman in her forties and to Carol, who was gazing down in wonder at the new arrival, she said, 'Well done! I take it that it was a fast birth.'

She grimaced.

'Too fast for comfort, but what a result!'

While the paramedics clamped and cut the cord and then supervised the ejection of the placenta, Alexa looked on wordlessly. If they hadn't arrived at that moment she would have had to cope as best as she could under the circumstances, so their appearance had been heaven sent.

'We're taking you both to hospital so that you can be checked over,' they told the new mother, who now that the crisis was over was becoming tearful. 'You've probably been in slow labour ever since the false alarm and not been aware of it.'

'I want Tom,' Carol bubbled. 'Where is he?'

'I know you do,' Alexa said gently. 'I'll leave a note for him explaining what's happened and I'll stay with you until he comes.'

'I don't know what I'd have done without you, Alexa,' her sister said with tears still threatening.

'It was something I will never forget,' she told her.

When an ecstatic Tom arrived at the hospital Alexa quietly left the room, leaving them to their special moment, and it was only then, as she made her way out of the maternity unit, that she came down to earth.

Her watch said it was ten minutes past ten and she froze. It was over an hour since she'd been about to go down to the lake to say goodbye to Reece.

When she hadn't appeared he would have decided that her 'maybe' had become a 'no', she thought dismally, and she knew instinctively that he would have taken it as final.

Helpless tears ran down her cheeks. The fates had been against her from the start. Why should they start favouring her now?

Yet it didn't stop her from rushing down to the lakeside the moment she got back, hoping for a miracle, but it was not to be. She was too late. There was just the water lapping against the shingle and a leaden sky above, which couldn't have been more appropriate for the occasion.

It was decided to keep mother and baby in hospital for a couple of days, and when Alexa and Tom went to see them that night the two women chatted while the proud father held his daughter.

'We're going to call her Amelia,' Carol said, 'after Tom's grandmother.'

'That's lovely,' Alexa said as tears threatened. They hadn't been far away ever since she'd stood on the deserted shore, but today of all days she didn't want to inflict her woes on Carol and Tom.

Fortunately they were too wrapped up in their new daughter to notice that the aunt who had brought her into the world was less than happy.

And after a quick cuddle with her new niece Alexa left them, knowing that soon she might take the edge off their joy with her own problems, which couldn't be shelved for much longer.

Baby Amelia was a week old and Carol a busy new mother, but it didn't stop her from noticing that Alexa was very quiet.

'What's happened to my bubbly young sister?' she asked one morning as Alexa was listlessly looking on while she fed the baby.

'She's maturing fast,' she said flatly.

'It's Reece, isn't it?' Carol probed gently. 'You're missing him dreadfully, aren't you?'

Alexa nodded. 'Yes. I am and yet, paradoxically, I was glad to see him go.'

'I can't believe that!' Carol exclaimed.

'It's true. I have a problem that I need to work out and I couldn't do it while he was here.'

'I'm not with you.'

'I'm pregnant, Carol. I'm carrying Reece's baby.'

'*What?*' She was aghast. 'And he's left you in that state? How could he?'

'He doesn't know.'

'I can't believe I'm hearing this. You've let him go without telling him?'

'I had to. If I'd told him he would have stayed.'

'But that's what you wanted.'

'Yes, it is, but not on those terms. As far as I'm concerned, for Reece to have changed his plans it would have to be for one reason only...that he couldn't bear to leave me. And, as he's now somewhere in the Middle East, events have shown that I didn't matter all that much.'

'I don't believe that,' Carol protested. 'The man was in love with you.'

'How do you know that I wasn't just a bit of light relief to make his break more pleasurable?'

'Because I know Reece Rowlinson. He's a man of complete integrity. Alexa, you can't deny him the knowledge that you're carrying his child.'

'Do you think I don't want to tell him,' she countered wretchedly. 'I would have loved to have told him, but that same integrity would have made him stay and I would have spent the rest of my life wondering if that was the only reason.'

She smiled down ruefully at the small downy head in the crook of her sister's arm.

'I'm sorry if I've put a blight on this happy time for you, Carol, but I had to tell you. Or my thickening waistline would have done it for me.'

'Come here,' Carol said gently. Putting her free arm around Alexa she said, 'I'm sorry about Reece's part in all this, and I know that he would be, too…if he knew. But won't it be lovely, our two little ones growing up together?'

'Yes, it will,' Alexa agreed tearfully.

It would, but nothing would ever seem right without Reece.

As Christmas drew nearer Alexa's condition was becoming known at the surgery. Not because it was showing, but the nausea *had* been noted, along with her general pallor, and they were all, of course, experienced in that kind of thing.

No one had asked outright who the father of her child was, but when someone meaningfully mentioned Robbie Durkin's name she felt compelled to make it clear that he wasn't the father.

But it didn't propel her into any further revelations. For one thing, if John found out he might get in touch with Reece and she didn't want that. Although there wasn't much likelihood of that at the moment as he was in hospital having an operation for the prostate cancer and would have more important things on his mind.

Beryl was the only one who knew that it was Reece's baby and she kept insisting, 'Tell the man. He has a right to know.'

But Alexa just shook her head.

'We're going to have Amelia christened at the carol service on the morning of Christmas Eve,' Carol said as they decorated the tree in the lofty hall of the guest house. 'Needless to say, you'll be godmother, if that's all right with you.'

'Of course it is,' Alexa beamed. 'But why so soon?'

'We want Tom's eldest brother as godfather and he's going to work in Saudi Arabia the moment Christmas is over.'

Her new niece was adorable. Every time she held her it was a promise of what was to come for herself, and if her child's future looked less rosy than Amelia's, it was something that its mother would have to accept.

It was hard to enter into the Christmas spirit with her heart as heavy as lead every time she thought about Reece, but she did her best. It was Carol's and Tom's first Christmas as a family and she didn't want her own misery to spoil it for them.

The staff at the practice had been out for their usual Christmas meal and, unable to refuse, she'd gone with them, but all the time she was remembering that the last time they'd been out together it had been Reece's farewell.

On the day before the christening Carol said, 'I've a confession to make, Alexa.'

'Oh? What is it?'

'I've written to the medical agency that Reece works for and asked them to forward a letter on to him.'

'You've what!'

'He has to know about the baby,' Carol said uncomfortably, 'and as you aren't prepared to tell him, I have.'

The colour had drained from Alexa's face.

'How could you? How could you do that to me, Carol?'

'I could do it because I can't bear to see you so unhappy. It isn't fair to him and it isn't fair to the baby either. Your health is going to suffer if you're in this state all the time you're pregnant...and you're hardly likely to bring a contented child into the world if you're depressed all the time you're carrying it.'

'And you think that bringing Reece back because he

feels guilty is going to sort out the mess my life is in?' she cried angrily.

'I'm sorry if I've upset you, Alexa,' Carol said firmly, 'but it had to be done. You need him.'

'And how long is it since you sent this letter?'

'As soon as you told me about the baby.'

As she walked slowly back to her own apartment Alexa admitted to herself that Carol was right about one thing. She needed him. Needed him like she needed to breathe. But surely her sister saw that it wasn't as simple as that.

She had made herself face the fact that she would have to cope without him, and now Carol was trying to take away the choice.

Alexa never went near her beloved lake these days. The memories were too painful. When she and Reece had first met it had been the focal point of their attraction, the place that held them in thrall. But now it stood for the futility of all that had gone between them.

They'd been happy beside it, passionate beside it, and angry, too, but now travelling to work on one of the frequent passenger ferries was the last thing she could face.

It was the same everywhere they'd been together. He was there. Like a tantalising shadow that never materialised.

The church was bright with Christmas cheer when they arrived for Amelia's christening, and Alexa thought what a suitable day it was for the event.

Baptisms took place in the middle of the morning service and today was to be no exception. They were seated in the front pew—Carol, Tom, his brother and his wife, and herself.

As the first carol rang out Alexa heard the door at the back of the church open and shut and thought absently that someone had been running late. But she took little notice.

Two things were occupying her mind. One was the tiny cherub in her arms, and the other was the determination not to become weepy when she made her responses.

When it was time for the christening they walked up to the front, and as she faced the congregation Alexa almost dropped her tiny niece.

Reece was sitting in a pew at the back. As his familiar dark gaze locked with hers the vicar asked for the name of the baptismal infant and after that it was just a blur.

Carol hadn't noticed Reece while the baptism was taking place, but she espied him as they went back to their seats and her smile said that she'd known he would come.

As the congregation gathered round the newly christened infant at the end of the service, Alexa walked slowly towards the solitary figure sitting at the back of the church.

'Hello, Alexa,' he said quietly as she hovered at the end of the pew. 'Are you surprised to see me?'

'Er…yes…I mean no.'

He smiled, but there was gravity in it rather than pleasure.

'Do you think we could go outside for a while? I'm sure that Carol and Tom wouldn't mind.'

She didn't answer, just walked blindly out into the quiet churchyard where a winter sun was struggling through. But once out there she found her voice.

'You didn't *have* to come.'

The grave smile was there again. 'That's not a very warm welcome.'

'I know the reason why you're here and Carol had no right to do what she did.'

He was observing her consideringly.

'You don't seem very pleased to see me,' he said levelly, ignoring the comment about her sister.

'I'm overjoyed to see you,' she said raggedly, 'but

it's the reason for you being here that I'm not happy about.

'That seems to me to be a contradiction in terms.'

'And you know why, don't you?' she said woodenly.

The churchgoers were beginning to drift outside and, taking her arm, Reece propelled her to a far part of the churchyard where they wouldn't be disturbed.

'We seem to be talking in riddles,' he said as they stopped beneath the bare branches of a tree.

'Please, don't pretend you haven't come back because of Carol's letter,' Alexa pleaded. 'I know that's why you're here. Her writing to you has brought about the very thing I wanted to avoid. I never wanted you to come back to me because of the baby.'

She saw his face change colour and his jaw slacken.

'Baby!' he echoed in wonderment. 'You're pregnant?'

'Yes. I am. That's why you've come back, isn't it? Because Carol wrote and told you.'

He shook his head, still dazed at the news.

'No. It isn't. I haven't received any letter from your sister. When did she send it?'

'Last weekend,' Alexa told him. Now it was her turn to be transfixed.

'Mail doesn't reach where I've come from as quickly as *that*.' His voice lifted. 'Alexa, I'm here for no other reason than I can't bear to be away from you. The moment I landed at the other end I knew I'd made a dreadful mistake even though you couldn't be bothered to say goodbye.'

She had lowered herself slowly on to a wooden bench and was gazing at him, wide-eyed.

'There was a good reason why I didn't show up at the lake, Reece. I was delivering Carol's baby at the time I should have been with you. She went into the fastest labour I've ever seen. I flew down there as fast as I could, but it was long after the appointed time and you'd gone.'

'So that was it,' he said softly. 'I would have come look-ing for you, but I was so sure you'd given up on me there seemed no point.'

So far they hadn't touched, but now he was holding his hand out to her and bringing her to her feet. In the second before his mouth came down on to hers Alexa saw what she'd longed to see.

It was there in his eyes. A deep abiding love. Love that he'd fought against for what had seemed like very good reasons, until they'd been apart. Now it had brought him back to her.

'What about the job?' she breathed some minutes later. 'You haven't just walked out on it, have you?'

He smiled and there was pure contentment in it.

'I think you know me better than that. I had to wait until they sent out a replacement.'

Suddenly he was serious.

'I've made my contribution to world health care, even if I were never to go out there again. But maybe one day when this little one...' he laid his hand gently on her stom-ach '...and any others that might follow have grown up, we could go back there. How would you feel about that, Alexa?'

The hazel eyes that for so long had been dull and lifeless were sparkling again as she told him, 'How I've felt from the moment I met you. That where you are, I need to be.'

Amelia's christening party was over. The star of the show was fast asleep in her cot, quite unaware that it had been her special day.

Her parents were clearing up after the event and her dot-ing aunt was making her way to where Derwentwater glis-tened in the cold winter night.

Reece had been warmly welcomed back into the fold by Carol and Tom and their friends from the practice, and would be staying with Alexa until he found a position more local than the one he'd just changed his mind about.

He'd left the party before her, saying as he went, 'I'l meet you at our special place in ten minutes.'

She'd nodded, her eyes alight with happiness, and now she was there. In the place that had a magic of its own for them, even on a dark December night.

When he heard her footsteps on the shingle, Reece turned away from his contemplation of the lake and held out his arms. And as she went into them like a bird to its nest, the waters at their feet lapped approvingly against the shore.

Modern Romance™
...seduction and
passion guaranteed

Tender Romance™
...love affairs that
last a lifetime

Sensual Romance™
...sassy, sexy and
seductive

Blaze
...sultry days and
steamy nights

Medical Romance™
...medical drama on
the pulse

Historical Romance™
...rich, vivid and
passionate

29 new titles every month.

*With all kinds of Romance for
every kind of mood...*

MILLS & BOON®

Makes any time special™

MAT4

MILLS & BOON®

Medical Romance™

GUILTY SECRET by Josie Metcalfe

Part 2 of Denison Memorial Hospital

It started the moment Nick set eyes on Dr Frances Long. More than sexual, it was soul deep. Then Frankie was introduced to the surgery's new GP—her colleague's fiancé, Nick Johnson! Frankie couldn't live with the guilt and neither could Nick. But until they were free to be together, how could anyone live happily ever after?

PARTNERS BY CONTRACT by Kim Lawrence

Dr Phoebe Miller is settling in well to her new practice —until senior partner Dr Connor Carlyle returns from his holiday and sparks begin to fly! Connor was Phoebe's first love, but he'd been bound to another woman. Now Connor is free again he wants to keep Phoebe as his partner in the practice—and in his life!

MORGAN'S SON by Jennifer Taylor

As Morgan stood by her bed with Tomàs in his arms Katrina felt her dream of adopting Tomàs with Morgan, and reviving their marriage after four years, evaporate. Morgan had always opposed adoption and her only hope had been to persuade him gently, slowly. Little chance of that now—unless Tomàs had worked his charms on Morgan too…

On sale 1st February 2002

0102/03a

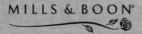

MILLS & BOON®

Medical Romance™

A VERY TENDER PRACTICE *by Laura MacDonald*

Life hasn't always been easy for Maggie. As a single mother and local GP, she has to be a survivor. Her determination has won her many admirers, but she never thought senior partner Sam would be one of them. Maggie begins to wonder if she can let go of her protective barriers enough to make him one of the family...

THE DOCTORS' MARRIAGE *by Leah Martyn*

When Dr Riley Brennan decided to work abroad as a volunteer doctor he'd wanted his wife Jane to go with him. However, she'd wanted a family, and when they couldn't agree he went alone. Now Riley's tracked Jane down and they'll be working together again. He's determined to save their marriage—even if it means seducing his wife all over again!

THE EMERGENCY ASSIGNMENT *by Carol Marinelli*

Consultant Samuel Donovan is not pleased when a film crew arrive at Melbourne Central to make a documentary on A&E. Erin Casey is in charge—and she's a big distraction. To Samuel at least! Erin soon falls hard for the irresistible Dr Donovan, but why does he think he's not husband material?

On sale 1st February 2002

Treat yourself this Mother's Day to the ultimate indulgence

3 brand new romance novels and a box of chocolates

= *only £7.99*

Available from 18th January

2 FREE

books and a surprise gift!

We would like to take this opportunity to thank you for reading this Mills & Boon® book by offering you the chance to take TWO more specially selected titles from the Medical Romance™ series absolutely FREE! We're also making this offer to introduce you to the benefits of the Reader Service™—

- ★ FREE home delivery
- ★ FREE gifts and competitions
- ★ FREE monthly Newsletter
- ★ Exclusive Reader Service discount
- ★ Books available before they're in the shops

Accepting these FREE books and gift places you under no obligation to buy, you may cancel at any time, even after receiving your free shipment. Simply complete your details below and return the entire page to the address below. *You don't even need a stamp!*

YES! Please send me 2 free Medical Romance books and a surprise gift. I understand that unless you hear from me, I will receive 4 superb new titles every month for just £2.49 each, postage and packing free. I am under no obligation to purchase any books and may cancel my subscription at any time. The free books and gift will be mine to keep in any case.

M2ZEA

Ms/Mrs/Miss/Mr ....Initials...............................
BLOCK CAPITALS PLEASE

Surname ....

Address ....

....

....Postcode...............................

Send this whole page to:
UK: FREEPOST CN81, Croydon, CR9 3WZ
EIRE: PO Box 4546, Kilcock, County Kildare (stamp required)